BEAST

FACE-TO-FACE WITH THE FLORIDA BIGFOOT

BOOKS BY WATT KEY

BEAST

FACE-TO-FACE WITH THE FLORIDA BIGFOOT

WATT KEY

FARRAR STRAUS GIROUX
NEW YORK

Farrar Straus Giroux Books for Young Readers
An imprint of Macmillan Publishing Group, LLC
120 Broadway, New York, NY 10271

Printed in the United States of America by LSC Communications,
Harrisonburg, Virginia
Designed by Sammy Yuen
First edition, 2020

1 3 5 7 9 10 8 6 4 2

mackids.com

Library of Congress Control Number: 2019943446
ISBN: 978-0-374-31369-2

Our books may be purchased in bulk for promotional, educational, or business use.
Please contact your local bookseller or the Macmillan Corporate and Premium Sales Department at
(800) 221-7945 ext. 5442 or by email at MacmillanSpecialMarkets@macmillan.com.

Special thanks to Cheairs Porter, Stephen Davis, Wes Germer, Andrew Gude, and Daniel Barrand for their help with this project

BEAST

FACE-TO-FACE WITH THE FLORIDA BIGFOOT

A LOT OF PEOPLE WANT TO KNOW WHERE I WAS FOR THE TWO months I went missing. And I know I've said I don't remember. I do remember—I just thought no one would believe me if I told them. Now I feel like I owe an explanation to everyone who helped me recover, especially Uncle John and Dr. Ensley and the people who found me nearly dead on the roadside. So I'm going to write it all here exactly as it happened. You'll probably think I'm crazy. I'm not. I know what I experienced. And I'm certain one day you too will see these things yourself and experience terror so great you'll want to die to escape it.

• • •

It all started with the accident. When I woke in the hospital, Sergeant Daniels was standing over my bed. He was tall and bulky and serious looking with his state trooper hat casting a shadow across my sheets. He told me my parents were missing, which made my head start throbbing even more than it already was. I had to close my eyes and take a few deep breaths. When I opened them again, he took a notepad and pen from his shirt pocket and asked me to try to remember everything that had happened. So I did.

We'd been to Disney World down in Orlando for a few days and were late getting back because of construction on Interstate 75. I was in the back seat of Dad's Jeep Cherokee. Right before it happened, I remember noticing the digital clock on the dashboard reading 1:11 a.m. We'd been off the interstate for nearly an hour, driving Highway 98 toward our home in Perry, Florida. Mom was asleep against the window of the passenger seat. I wasn't supposed to be awake, but seeing Dad driving so quiet and alone on the empty highway made me uneasy.

"Then there was something in the road," I said to the state trooper. "Dad turned the wheel and then I don't remember anything else."

"What was in the road?" the trooper asked me.

The question made me see flashes of something. Like a movie playing with scenes missing. Scenes I didn't want to remember.

"I don't know," I said.

"Like a tire? A bag of trash?"

The movie flashed in my head again, and I closed my eyes and forced it away.

"I don't know," I said again.

"How big was it?"

I shook my head. The trooper waited, his pen hovering over the notepad.

"You said something was in the road," he continued. "There's no report of any obstacles on the highway at the scene."

"It was standing in the road," I said.

"Then it was an animal? A deer maybe? There's lots of deer in the hammock."

I shook my head. "It wasn't a deer."

"A wild pig? Maybe it was a wild pig."

"It was standing," I said.

The trooper studied me, not writing anything. "You mean on two legs?"

I nodded.

He lowered his pen.

"A person?"

I didn't want to describe what I'd seen. I didn't want to remember it at all.

"Son, was there a person standing in the road?"

Then I couldn't keep my thoughts to myself with the trooper towering over me and staring at me like he was.

"It was right there in our headlights. It looked like a man. But it wasn't. It was too big. It was as tall as a basketball goal, and its shoulders were as wide as three men put together. Its arms hung down to its knees, and it was covered with black hair. Everything was covered with hair except for the face. It had a man's face. Except for the eyes. The eyes were black too."

Relief settled over me. Surely the trooper could give me the answer to what it was I'd seen that night.

"Like a bear?" he said.

The momentary relief I'd felt vanished. I shook my head. Suddenly I felt like crying.

"It wasn't a bear," I said.

"There's black bears out there. And they can stand up."

"It wasn't a bear," I said weakly.

The trooper started to say something else, but didn't. Then he lifted his pen and started to write, but stopped. He put the pen away and lowered the notepad.

"You don't know what it was, do you?" I said.

"I think maybe you need to get some more rest. Then we can talk about it again later."

"Did they find my parents yet?"

"No," he said. "But they're still searching the river."

"But you think they're dead."

He hesitated. "We don't know that yet."

• • •

The day after my visit with the trooper, there was a short article in the local paper.

COUPLE MISSING AFTER CRASH; BOY RESCUED

FANNING SPRINGS — On Sunday morning at approximately 1:00 a.m., a Jeep Cherokee traveling westbound on US Highway 98 sideswiped a telephone pole and swerved off the roadway, plunging into the Suwannee River west of Fanning Springs. The driver was Adam Parks, 43, of Perry, Florida. Passengers were his wife, Hazel Parks, 44, and their thirteen-year-old son, Adam Jr. Emergency personnel were unable to locate the parents. Search and rescue efforts in the area are underway. The doors of the vehicle were all open, and the boy was found unconscious at the side of the road. He was treated at the scene and transported to Chiefland Medical Center, where he is in stable condition. According to the boy, the family was returning from a trip to Disney World in Orlando. He has told police his father swerved to avoid a collision with a Sasquatch-like creature standing in the highway. A state police spokesperson said they had no comment at this time.

A Sasquatch-like creature. Those were their words, not mine. I didn't even know the word *Sasquatch*. Had I known the problems it would cause—just the suggestion I'd seen such a thing—I would have never opened my mouth about it.

2

EVEN THOUGH I HAD BEEN FOUND UNCONSCIOUS, THE DOCTORS
at the hospital said the tests they ran on me all came up
negative for concussion. It seemed my injuries were limited
to cuts on my face and bruises, but the doctors kept me in
the hospital to monitor for internal bleeding. Sergeant
Daniels didn't visit me again, but Mom's brother, Uncle
John, came by as much as he could. I guess he'd gotten
there within hours of them bringing me in.

If my parents were really gone, Uncle John would be
the last of my close family. He had Mom's same thick
brown hair and wide eyes. He was six-and-a-half-feet tall,
a little overweight and socially awkward. He'd never
gotten married and lived alone in Cross City, a small com-
munity just fifteen miles west of Fanning Springs. He was

a control board operator at Florida Power and Light Company.

It was Uncle John who showed me the newspaper article. Considering that it said his nephew had reported seeing a Sasquatch, I figured he might want to talk about it, but he didn't. He was known for his corny jokes, but now he didn't seem to want to talk much about anything. I think he was as stunned as I was over the situation with my parents.

"Adam and Hazel just always did everything right," he said. "They were the best of us all."

As their son I guess I took them for granted and might never have thought that before, but now that they weren't around, I could see it was true. Our family may not have seemed particularly special at first glance. Dad ran a small insurance company, and Mom was his receptionist and bookkeeper. We went to church most Sundays and took a trip to Disney World once a year. Dad was the volunteer coach for my Little League team. He liked to read and garden and walk in the woods. Mom cooked for the school bake sale fund-raisers. She enjoyed jogging and eighties pop music, and sometimes I caught her dancing when she didn't think anyone was looking. It was all so boringly normal, but I guess that's what made it so happy and safe.

When I was six, Uncle John talked Dad into joining the Cabbage Hammock hunting club in Dixie County. Dad wasn't into the deer hunting aspect of it, but he liked to cook for the camp members and walk with me in the woods and talk to me about the plants and animals. This was his idea of a good day in the woods. At first I was disappointed he didn't own a powerful deer rifle like Uncle John and the others. That he didn't shoot big bucks and hang the mounted heads on the walls at our house. All he had was a Ruger 222, and he let me carry it on our walks and try to shoot squirrels.

When I was eight I finally brought home a squirrel I'd shot at the hunting camp. I skinned and cleaned it in the kitchen like Dad showed me and put the meat in the freezer. Then I took the hide into my room and spread it on a board and nailed it down. I poured Morton salt over it to cure it so I could make a hat. After a week Mom trailed the smell and found my project under the bed. When I got home from school, she had placed it outside and asked me about it. I couldn't tell if she approved or not, so I said I was making her a purse, assuming she couldn't turn down a gift. The next day I took it off the board and sewed the feet pieces together with a big needle and dental floss until I had a squirrel-hide pouch complete with tail. Then I used a piece of red yarn to make a shoulder strap. Mom wore it over her shoulder to church that Sunday, smell and all.

That's how she was.

When I was twelve, Dad bought a deer rifle. I thought he was going to finally shoot a buck, and I wanted to be with him when he did. We got dressed in the early morning hours and walked to our stand. Sometimes it takes an entire season to get a shot, but we hadn't been there thirty minutes before an eight point appeared ghostlike out of the misty timber. It was like Dad had been saving it for us all those years. But then he slipped the rifle to me and told me to remember how I'd shot the squirrel. To aim for the shoulder and hold my breath and squeeze the trigger. I killed the buck, and he told me the rifle was mine.

That's how he was.

• • •

Late Monday afternoon Uncle John brought me an iPad so I could stream movies and browse the internet while I was recovering. It didn't take me long to find video footage from a local news crew on the scene of our accident. A female reporter stood in the midst of strobing blue and red lights talking about the crash, while behind her a wrecker winched Dad's Jeep from the river. As it came up the bank, slime covered and dripping, I saw that the doors were hanging open and the back window was missing.

I brought up a map of the area. The accident happened just north of the Suwannee National Wildlife Refuge, nearly fifty thousand acres of swampy hammock. The Suwannee River cut down the center of the refuge clear to its mouth at the Gulf of Mexico. It was overwhelming just staring at the map, thinking my parents were somewhere out in that vastness, alive, or not.

I turned off the tablet and just lay there in the darkened room. I couldn't sleep, but I didn't want to be awake either.

Even though they were still considered missing, I knew in my gut they were gone for good. I couldn't admit it, but I knew it. And when I tried to imagine life without them, my thoughts went blank and I got a faint ringing in my ears. I couldn't even think about it. My mind wasn't able to go there yet.

How? I kept asking myself. *How can this happen?*

I kept trying to make sense of things, but it was like my brain had turned to mush. All I could do was stare at the wall while bits and pieces of what I'd gone through the night of the wreck kept flashing past like bits of broken glass.

A Sasquatch-like creature.

I kept seeing the beast in my head. I knew it wasn't a bear or anything else I'd ever laid eyes on.

After hours in the dark, I suddenly found myself desperate to focus on something other than my thoughts and the flashing movie scenes. I grabbed the iPad, opened the browser, and did a Google search for Sasquatch. It took me only a moment to see this creature mostly went by a name I *had* heard of. Bigfoot.

3

IF ANYTHING'S CLEAR IT'S THAT BIGFOOT IS NOT A HIDDEN
creature on the internet. Just searching that word alone,
the results page listed almost fifty million hits. I clicked
on some blurry videos and pictures before I found a site for
the Bigfoot Searchers Organization. The BSO, as they like
to call it, seemed to have the most clear and organized information about the creatures. I quickly discovered people all
over the country—all over the world—had been seeing them
since the beginning of recorded history. There was even an
online map showing all the reported sightings in each state.
Florida alone had hundreds. Levy County, where we'd had
the accident, had had twelve.

I began reading about some of the encounters. Most
were roadside sightings by motorists, but many reports

were from hunters and farmers. Sasquatch and Bigfoot were the most common names for the creatures, but I learned there are others, depending on what part of the country you're in. In Florida, it's often called a swamp ape in the Panhandle area and a skunk ape around the Everglades. People claim they carry a powerful smell that's something like week-old roadkill crossed with rotten eggs. The adults are typically between six and twelve feet tall, their bodies broad and muscular, and estimated to weigh six hundred to a thousand pounds. While all the eyewitnesses generally describe a giant apelike man, there are subtle differences. Some of the reports claim to have seen a creature that is more apelike, with eyes that glow red. Others describe what I had seen clearly in the headlights: the face of a Neanderthal with black eyes staring through a mane of hair. Despite varying names and appearances, the creatures all have one main thing in common: big footprints.

As I read on into the night, I began to realize why so few people talk about Bigfoot. Despite all the sightings, there is no convincing proof it really exists. It's a cryptid: an animal whose existence has never been substantiated. Witnesses have the footprints and blurry videos and pictures, but that's all. To most people this creature is in the same category as aliens and chupacabras and the Mothman.

That night I had dreams more vivid and terrifying

than any I'd ever experienced. I woke several times in a cold sweat, lying in the quiet semidarkness, breathing hard, listening to the faint chirping and beeping of hospital equipment beyond my walls. What was strange about the nightmares is they weren't scary in a "deadly animals attacking me" kind of way. It was a smothering fear they filled me with, a feeling of being absolutely alone in a world that suddenly wasn't at all what I'd been taught about it. A fear I'd gotten a glimpse of something I wasn't supposed to see, that perhaps I was going to be punished for. And the growing realization I could no longer trust anything adults told me.

• • •

I didn't sleep soundly until after the sun came up Tuesday morning. Daylight always seems to ease my fears, and it did so enough to let me drift off again until the nurse came to change my bandages a few hours later. Then Uncle John dropped by again with Krispy Kreme doughnuts and sat there and ate a couple with me.

"You look a little red in the eyes," he said.

"I didn't sleep good," I said.

"Yeah, me neither. Doc Ensley says you might be out of here tomorrow."

"Okay."

"Says it's a miracle you weren't hurt worse."

I nodded.

"There's no word on your parents yet."

"I know," I said.

After he left I slept again but found the nightmares were stronger than daylight. They crawled all over me. This time I dreamt I was walking through our house in the middle of the night. I looked into my parents' bedroom, and they weren't in bed. Then I went over to their closet and opened it, and they were in there, lifeless, hooked up to some kind of charger with their eyes blinking. I ran out into the yard to get help, and everything was turned off, like I was the only real person in the world and everybody and everything else was a trick.

I woke up yelling. A nurse came in and stood over me and asked if I was okay.

"No," I said.

"Do you need the doctor?"

I shook my head. I wanted to cry. "No," I said again.

She held out a pill.

"Here you go, hun," she said. "This'll help you forget about that monster."

I looked at her. She didn't believe me either. But at the moment I wanted to sleep without nightmares more than I cared what people believed. So I took the pill, and whatever it was, it was stronger than my dreams.

4

UNCLE JOHN AND I WALKED OUT OF THE HOSPITAL LATE
Wednesday morning, and I felt sunlight on my face for the
first time in nearly four days. I'm sure I looked a mess,
with some of the bandages visible on my nose and left
cheek. My entire body was sore and tight from bruises and
stitches, but otherwise I felt physically fine. It was my
mind that was still sick.

I climbed into the passenger side of his truck. He told
me we were going to Perry to get whatever things I needed
from the house. Then I was coming to live with him until
we learned more about my parents.

"What about school?" I said.

"I've made arrangements for you to attend in Cross
City. Just for now. Just until we know more. They're

searching the entire Refuge. Both sides of the river clear down to the mouth and out into the Gulf."

"I don't think they could have lived out there for this long," I said.

Uncle John looked at me. "Adam, I'm not giving up on them, but we'll have to face reality at some point. Chances are they're not coming back. That's a dangerous river. The current's strong. The water's dark. There's alligators and snakes all over the place."

I looked out the window.

"We simply don't know what happened and may never know," he said.

"What if they don't find them?"

"Your parents had a will. They left you in my care, and I intend to do the best job I can raising you."

I looked back at him again. "That's not what I mean. I mean, how do you have a funeral?"

"Well, you just have one anyway. There's just, you know . . ."

"Empty graves?"

"We don't need to talk about that yet. I think it's best if we both try to get ourselves together and press on."

"I don't know if I can," I said.

Uncle John looked over at me. "You'll be okay, Adam. It won't be easy, but people live through this stuff."

"I can't sleep," I said. "I have bad dreams. Even in the daytime."

"Okay," he said, thoughtfully. "I'll see about finding someone you can talk to about it."

"Nobody knows anything," I said.

"What do you mean? There's doctors that specialize in helping people with this kind of stuff."

I shook my head. "They don't know about what happened to me. About my nightmares and what I saw."

Uncle John sighed. "Is this about the Sasquatch?"

I hated the word. He didn't mean it, but I heard the mockery in his voice.

I looked out the window again. "Never mind," I said.

"You probably saw a bear, Adam. It was dark and easy to get confused."

"Okay," I said. "I was just . . . I don't know. I don't want to talk about it anymore."

"There's no such thing as Sasquatch."

I looked at him. "I'd never even heard that word," I said. "The newspaper called it that, not me."

"Then what did you tell them?" he asked.

"I told the state trooper what I saw."

"How do you know it wasn't a bear?"

I couldn't hold back my anger and frustration. "It

wasn't a bear!" I shouted. "I know what I saw, and it wasn't a bear!"

Uncle John studied the road, looking a little startled. "Okay," he said. "No problem. I believe you."

I took a few deep breaths and tried to calm myself.

"Listen," he said, finally. "I believe you think you saw this thing. I do."

"Forget it," I mumbled.

"I'm going to tell you a story about something that happened to me when I was about your age. There was a boy who moved into my neighborhood who I got to be friends with. One day he asks me if I want to go to camp with him that summer. It was just this weeklong thing his church did. Your grandparents thought it sounded okay, and it wasn't expensive so I went. Turned out it was some kind of extreme Bible camp. The preacher put his hand on these kids' heads and told them he was sending Jesus into them. They started flipping about on the ground and shouting all this weird stuff. Speaking in tongues, they call it."

"So you're saying I'm crazy?"

"No, I'm not saying that. I'm saying, depending on people's state of mind, they can believe what they want to believe."

He thought I was nuts. I supposed everybody did.

"You think I want to believe in Bigfoot?" I said.

"Look, let's just forget it for now."

"I don't want any of this."

"I know," he said. "I know."

•••

We pulled up in front of my home in the Glen Oaks sub-division. There wasn't much to it: a three-bedroom wood-frame house that looked pretty much like all the others. We'd lived there for as long as I could remember. For a moment I thought it was possible my parents would be inside waiting for me—that it was all a big misunder-standing. But that flash of hope quickly disappeared when I saw Mom's car in the driveway sprinkled with oak leaves and that the windows of the house were dark.

Uncle John had a spare key and walked with me to the front door and let me in. Then he waited in the foyer while I went back to my room. It was strange being in there, the house just like we'd left it, smelling like Mom and Dad. When I entered my room, it felt like entering a tomb full of ancient artifacts—items left long ago by some kid that wasn't alive anymore.

I didn't want much. I grabbed my L.L.Bean school backpack and slung it over my shoulder. I got my Treblehook Gear fishing cap off the bedpost and slipped it on. Then I pulled my duffel bag from under the bed and filled it with some extra clothes. At the last minute, I glanced at my dresser and saw the Swiss Army knife Dad had given me on my tenth birthday. I grabbed it and shoved it in my pocket. Then I turned and walked out and pulled the door shut behind me.

I didn't want to stay in there.

5

UNCLE JOHN'S HOUSE IS A SMALL BRICK HOME JUST ON THE
outskirts of Cross City. It's neat and tidy on the inside, but
it always gave me the sense it's a place where a man lives
alone. The furniture is basic and the rooms are mostly
bare of decorations. It has the overall smell of pine and
glue and laundry detergent. It's not unpleasant, but certainly not comforting.

I'd asked my parents once why Uncle John never had a
wife.

"Sometimes, if a person doesn't get married early, they
get too set in their ways to make it work later," Dad said.

"John had some opportunities," Mom continued, "but
they didn't work out for one reason or another."

I didn't get the sense they disapproved, but I could tell

they felt sorry for him. And I suppose it made *me* feel sorry for him, which bothered me. But it didn't seem like there was any purpose to him. Like he just spent his whole life in orbit between the power company and his house, and occasionally shooting out like a comet to the hunting camp during deer season. And that was just because he knew Dad and I were going to be there. He was friendly enough, but he didn't seem to have any friends. I didn't see how he'd ever replace Dad.

Uncle John had cleaned out his extra bedroom, which was used for storage. He'd furnished it with a bed frame, mattress, and small chest of drawers. Otherwise the room was a bare box with about as much character as a prison cell.

• • •

Uncle John told me the situation with my parents was still too uncertain for me to start school that week. If we hadn't heard anything by Sunday evening, then my first day at Cross City Middle would be Monday.

For the rest of the week, I rested during the day. Uncle John's shift didn't start until six o'clock in the evening, so he was at the house most of the day sleeping.

I stayed off the iPad and the internet. I lay on the living room sofa watching old reruns of Western movies during the day. It helped keep my mind distracted. But the nights were a different story. I tossed against visions of all things cryptid—vampires and werewolves and the Rake. And when I finally woke, I found myself yelling to an empty house.

After two nights of this, I asked Uncle John to get more sleeping pills for me. He picked up some melatonin at the grocery store, and it helped. He also made an appointment for me to see a therapist the following Wednesday. I wished there was a way to erase the horrors seared into my brain and start over. I didn't have any confidence I could be helped, but at that point I was willing to try anything.

• • •

We hadn't heard much in the way of news about my parents by Sunday evening. In response to Uncle John's phone calls, the police said the search was still ongoing, the investigation still open. On Monday morning I took my old schoolbooks out of my backpack so it was mostly empty. The week before our vacation to Disney World, my class had gone on a field trip to Wakulla Springs. Mom had bought a poncho and a disposable waterproof camera for me to take. We were going to be outside on a nature tour, and if the weather was bad the poncho would keep me drier than my rain jacket. The camera was for pictures with my friends, which she was always bugging me about.

It didn't rain, so the poncho was still unopened. I've never been much for taking photos, so I took only four, just enough to say I'd used it. There were still thirty-two exposures left. For some reason, now that Mom was gone, I felt guilty for not doing the simple things I knew made her happy. So I left the poncho and the camera in the pack, planning to use the remaining film, not sure that she would ever get to see the pictures. Then I bagged a lunch, slung my backpack over my shoulder, and left with Uncle John for Cross City Middle.

Back in Perry I'd been at the same school since kindergarten and knew just about everybody in my grade. I wasn't great at sports, and my grades were average. I wasn't supercool, but I wasn't a dork either. School has just always been pretty easy and comfortable. Here in Cross City, though, I was starting over.

I probably should have been nervous, but I wasn't. I was relieved I didn't have to see kids I knew. That I didn't have to listen to people say they were sorry about my parents and talk about the accident and the stupid newspaper article. Here in Cross City, I figured I could disappear for as long as I wanted.

The assistant principal gave me my books and a

schedule of my classes. Then he walked me to a home-room full of chatting kids and introduced me to the teacher. She was nice and looked over my schedule and gave me a map of the school and circled where my class-rooms were. Then I took a seat near the back of the room, thankful none of the other students seemed to notice me.

First period was math. I already knew what they were studying and tuned out most of it. English was next. The class was reading *The Red Pony* by John Steinbeck. The teacher gave me a copy and told me to catch up as soon as I could. After English we had a fifteen-minute break in the lunchroom. Then I went to history class. That's when the problems started.

The teacher's name was Mr. Thornton. At the begin-ning of the period, he had me come to the front of the room, stand in front of the whiteboard, and introduce myself. A classroom of nearly twenty students grew silent and stared at me.

"I'm Adam Parks," I said.

"Where are you from, Adam?" Mr. Thornton asked.

I felt myself getting uneasy. "Perry," I said.

"And what brings you to Cross City?"

"I just moved here," I said.

Then there was that boy. There's always that boy. And he's always big and likes to twiddle pencils in his mouth.

"What happened to your face?" the boy said, in a way that sounds innocent but you know it's not.

Half the class started chuckling.

"Shut up, Gantt!" a girl with blond hair snapped. "He was in a car accident."

I felt my heart drumming in my chest.

Mr. Thornton was already moving toward Gantt. He stood over him and motioned toward the door. "Out," he said. "Into the hall."

Some of the boys laughed. Gantt grinned and made a point of slowly standing up and grabbing his books. Then he strolled out of the room, still grinning.

"Is that true, Adam?" Mr. Thornton asked.

I nodded.

"I'm sorry to hear that. I hope everybody's okay."

"I saw it on the news," the girl said. "I hope they find your parents."

"I read about that in the paper!" a boy with red hair said. "You're the one that saw the swamp ape!"

Nobody was laughing now. I felt like I was about to puke. I left the whiteboard and started for the back of the room, as far back as possible.

"We're glad to have you, Adam," Mr. Thornton said after me. "And I'm sure your family will be in all of our prayers."

I took my seat in the back and stared at the cover of

my book. The queasiness had left me, and now my mouth was dry and my scalp tingled and a steady ringing sounded in my ears and made it impossible to think. Like my head was full of crawling, whining termites eating my brain. *I'm losing my mind now*, I thought. *This is what it feels like.*

I don't remember anything Mr. Thornton said for the next forty-five minutes. Then I vaguely realized class was over and got up and followed the others out into the hall. It was lunchtime, and everyone was going to their lockers. I hadn't gone far before I came across Gantt, who was standing with some other guys.

"Hey, Adam," he said in that fake-nice voice. "Tell me about the swamp ape."

I stopped and looked up at him. For a moment I just stood there, staring at his meaty face through the buzzing in my head.

"What'd it look like?" Gantt said.

One of the other boys snickered.

I dropped my backpack and tackled Gantt against the lockers. I heard kids yelling around me as I drove my fists into his stomach as hard as I could, over and over again. We fell sideways to the floor and I kept hitting him. Then he managed to roll me before he was suddenly pulled away by a teacher. I lay there, breathing hard, staring past a bunch of strange faces.

6

UNCLE JOHN HAD TO COME GET ME FROM SCHOOL. HE MET WITH the assistant principal in his office while I waited in the hall. After a few minutes he walked out frowning and motioned for me to follow him. It wasn't until we were crossing the parking lot that he said anything.

"Geez, Adam. What happened?"

"I don't want to talk about it," I said.

"You just got suspended from school on your first day. I think it's time to start talking about things."

I didn't respond.

We got into his truck and started for the house. We hadn't gone far before Uncle John's cell phone rang. He answered it.

"Yeah," he said. "Yeah, this is John Walker . . . Okay . . . Okay."

He slowed the truck and pulled onto the roadside. I looked over at him. He put the truck in park and sat back in his seat. He took a deep breath.

"So what's next?" he said into the phone.

I knew who it was.

"Okay . . . Please do. Thank you."

He set the phone down and rubbed his face. "They've called off the search," he said.

I didn't answer him. The words weren't any surprise. He looked at me. "They said something might still come up. If they find anything they'll contact us immediately. Who knows how long this could take?"

"We already know it's too late," I said. "We already know they're gone."

Uncle John put the truck into gear and didn't say anything. There was nothing to say. I looked out the window as my throat tightened and tears began rolling down my face. I just felt sick and ruined and hopeless.

• • •

Uncle John went to work that evening, and I was alone again. My parents were gone. I was suspended from school. Everyone thought I was crazy. *And what if I was?* I thought of something Dad had told me once. "Always be considerate. Crazy people don't know they're crazy."

How would I know it?

All I knew for certain is Mom's and Dad's disappearances and the vision of this creature had left me stunned. My world had been wiped clean. It didn't seem I had anything to live for except finding my way to the truth and figuring out where I fit into this world that wasn't at all what I'd been taught it would be like.

Was it real? Was Bigfoot a real thing or, as Uncle John said, something my mind had made up?

I got out the iPad again and went to the Bigfoot research site. These were my people now, crazy or not.

• • •

I read through report after report, this time focusing more on the witnesses than their encounters. The interviewers who compiled the reports gave a short assessment of the eyewitness's character at the end of each document. None of the assessments led me to believe these people were lying or crazy. Some were even doctors and lawyers and police officers.

While it was a relief to know there were others like me who had seen these things, and they didn't sound crazy, it wasn't enough. I needed to speak to one of these people. I needed to hear a voice tell me I wasn't losing my mind.

I thought about contacting the site and submitting my

own encounter. One of their investigators would contact me and then I could communicate with someone who would understand. Then I considered none of the reports were made by children or teenagers, and mine would certainly stand out. And maybe more people would connect me to the report since my story was so fresh in the news. That would just make things worse. There had to be another way.

I kept reading through all the Florida encounters. I came across one from another Panhandle town called Yellow Jacket, just south of Fanning Springs and only about twenty miles from Cross City. A man who lived on the edge of Suwannee National Wildlife Refuge claimed to have heard his cows lowing and running about his pasture at two o'clock in the morning. He got into his truck and drove out to the field to find all the cows bunched up in a corner, nearly climbing on top of one another. They were so frightened and packed so tightly against the electric fence, they'd short-circuited it. He drove into the pasture, and his headlight beams revealed a creature sitting next to a cedar tree eating the torn-off leg of one of his cows.

The report was submitted on June 11, 2013, and the encounter had happened in October of 1991. But I'd found most of the encounters weren't reported until years later. Like me, the witnesses hadn't known what they'd seen. And until they met or read about others who'd seen the same thing, they'd been scared to talk about it.

I searched the report, looking for information as to where exactly this farm was. It didn't list the man's name or address, but there were several clues. First of all, the location description read "approximately one mile south of Yellow Jacket on County Road 34." Second of all, there was the detail about the cedar tree. From the incident report it sounded like the tree would have been in the middle of the field. It seemed unusual to have a cedar tree in the middle of a cow pasture.

But even if I could find the location, I had no way of knowing if this man still lived there. The only thing I knew for sure is he was the closest opportunity for getting to the truth. I felt I had to find this farm and this man if I were to even begin putting my life back together again.

I made a desperate decision.

• • •

I figured it would take me most of the night to walk the twenty miles to Yellow Jacket. Of course Uncle John would discover I was gone the next morning, so I left a note to keep him from worrying too much.

Dear Uncle John,

I want you to know I am okay. I have gone looking for answers. I'll be back when I have them. Thank you for everything you've done, and please try not to worry about me.

Adam

7

I TOOK MY SCHOOLBOOKS OUT OF MY BACKPACK AND STUFFED it with an extra pair of jeans, a few pairs of socks, a flannel shirt, an undershirt, and a rain jacket. The temperature hadn't gotten below the midfifties, so I didn't think I needed more. Then I slipped on my fishing cap and stepped out of the room.

I stopped in the kitchen and checked my wallet. I counted twelve dollars. Then I rummaged through the kitchen and found a penlight, a few packages of peanut butter crackers, two cans of Vienna sausage, and three plastic bottles of water. I put these things in with the clothes, slung the backpack over my shoulder, and stepped out into the night.

• • •

There's not much to Cross City. It's basically a pass-through town with a population of no more than two thousand people. Once you get on the main highway and walk past two gas stations and a Dollar General, you're into the countryside. Then it's pine trees and palms on both sides of the blacktop and the occasional farmhouse and cow pasture.

The highway is mostly deserted that time of night. I plodded along the roadside, the sky clear and specked with stars. Frogs cheeped from the ditches, and crickets chirped from the scrub. Occasionally I heard the lonely call of an owl from a place even deeper into the forest. Just a week before, if you'd asked me to walk this road alone in the dark, I would have been frightened. Now I felt impervious to it all. Fear had been redefined for me.

It was almost one o'clock in the morning before I came to Highway 349, just outside of Fanning Springs. Had I kept walking another mile, I would have come to the site of the accident, but I didn't want to go there and dwell on it. I had to keep moving ahead. So I turned and started south on the road to Yellow Jacket, visualizing the Suwannee River edging closer and soon to be paralleling me from the east. Somewhere, between me and the river, was where the creature had walked.

Before the accident the Suwannee was little more to me than just another river we crossed over heading into south Florida. I'd heard the famous song about it, and in school we talked about the gulf sturgeon migrating up it in spring and leaving late fall. But the river was an hour away from Perry, so it wasn't a place I often considered. Occasionally there were stories in the news of people getting killed when their boats collided with leaping sturgeon, but I didn't give them much thought. The dangers of the Suwannee just weren't anything I ever expected to encounter. Little did I know just how mysterious and vast the scope of these dangers were.

· · ·

There were no houses on the road to Yellow Jacket, and I didn't pass a single car. My watch showed four o'clock in the morning when I arrived at a crossroads. There wasn't even a stop sign. The only indication I'd arrived was a sign for County Road 34, pointing down a sandy dirt road into a pine plantation. I walked about a mile before the pines suddenly ended and I saw an overgrown pasture to my left. Even if there had been a cedar tree in the middle of it, there was no way to see through the wild tangle of cabbage palms, palmetto, briars, and brambles.

I kept walking until I came to a driveway that led into a two-acre cutout of the old field. I saw a farmhouse with a single light glowing over the front porch. To the left of the house was what looked like a barn, and I reasoned this was as good a place as any to start. But I was tired, and it was too late and dark to be creeping around a stranger's property. It would have to wait until morning. So I lay down on the roadside and used my backpack as a pillow. Then I closed my eyes and slept without nightmares for the first time since I'd left the hospital.

• • •

I woke to the sun shining over the treetops onto my face. I looked at my watch and saw it was just past eight o'clock in the morning. I sat up and studied the farmhouse. It was wood framed and mostly gray where the paint had flaked off. To the left was a barn with some of the roof collapsed. There was a rusty pickup truck with flat tires in the side yard. Had there not been a light on behind the front windows, I would have thought the place abandoned.

I approached the house and stopped before it. There was a ramp at one end of the porch and concrete steps in the middle. I studied the windows and listened but didn't hear anything. I walked up the steps onto the porch, and boards creaked underfoot as I approached the front door. Then I knocked and waited. Nothing. After a moment I knocked again. Still nothing. I stepped sideways and peered into a window.

"Hello?" I called out.

There was no answer. I knocked again. I thought I heard the floor creaking from inside.

"Hello?" I said again.

"What do you want!" a man shouted.

"I'm Adam Parks from Cross City," I said.

"I'm not buying anything, and I don't have a phone!"

"I'm not here to sell anything, and I don't need to call anybody. I just want to ask you a question."

"Then ask me."

"Are you the one that wrote in about Bigfoot?"

"I don't know what you're talking about."

"In 2013. Someone reported they'd seen one nearby in 1991."

"The answer's no. Get off my property."

"Did you live here in 1991?"

"That's two questions."

"Did you hear about it?"

"That's three questions. Get out of here before I stick a shotgun in your face."

I wasn't convinced the man was telling the truth, but I didn't know what else to do besides travel farther down the road and look for another house. I stepped off the porch and walked into the yard and stopped and looked around. Something caught my eye to the right. I studied an overgrown patch of cabbage palms and palmetto. In the midst of it were the rusty remains of a tractor. I slowly turned and studied the edges of the yard, staring deep into the underbrush. And I began to see more. There was the black outline of a rotten cattle chute. There was an aluminum cattle gate that seemed to lead to nowhere. I looked at the barn again. On the second story a hayloft door hung open like it had been stuck that way for years. This place had definitely been a cattle farm once. And if I really wanted to make sure it was the right one, somewhere out in that overgrown field would be the large cedar tree.

8

I WENT BACK TO THE ROAD IN CASE THE MAN WAS WATCHING
me. Then I walked out of sight of the driveway and stepped
off into the thicket. I remembered something Dad told me
on one of our walks in the woods. He said if you wanted
to go in a straight line, find a big tree in the distance and
walk toward it. If there weren't any trees, you could rely on
the sun, making small adjustments for its westerly movement. In this case there were no big trees to be seen. I kept
the sun over my right shoulder and started fighting my
way through the underbrush.

It didn't take me long to intersect what looked like a
deer trail heading in the same general direction. By duck-
ing down I was able to make easier progress. I went another
hundred yards, and the brush thinned enough for me to

stand and peer into the treetops. And I saw it off to my right, the evergreen canopy of the cedar rising out of the tangled ruin.

As I approached the lost cedar, an eerie feeling fell over me. It seemed there was still something of the creature's presence lingering ghostlike in this place. I imagined the old pasture as it must have been years before, lush and green. I pictured the creature sitting beneath this very same tree, eating from the cow leg.

I ran my hand over the bark and sat next to it, thinking perhaps I was sitting in the very place the creature had been. I leaned against the trunk and looked up into the canopy. If only this tree could tell me what it had seen. But I felt I was getting closer now. A calm settled over me, and I closed my eyes and slept again.

• • •

When I woke it was late afternoon, and the air was getting cooler. Now I knew this was the right place, but I still didn't know if I'd found the right man. He could be someone new who had moved here. There was only one way to find out.

I approached the farmhouse again. This time I didn't knock. I knew he heard me crossing the porch, and I knew he was listening.

"I saw one," I said.

There was no response.

"He was in the road near Fanning Springs. People think I'm crazy. I just wanted to talk to somebody."

A few moments of silence followed. Then I heard a commotion inside. The door opened, and the man was sitting before me in a wheelchair. He looked to be about seventy years old. His face was tan and lined, like he'd spent a lifetime in the sun. His hair was white and wispy and tied into a ponytail.

"I just want to know what it is," I said.

He studied me for a moment. "I don't get many visitors."

"I won't stay long. I'll stay out here on the porch if you want."

The man frowned and backed the wheelchair away from the door. "Come inside," he said.

• • •

The farmhouse reminded me of our hunting cabin. It was made out of rough-sawn, untreated pine and smelled like turpentine and mothballs. The furniture was old and wooden, with the varnish worn off in all places a hand would touch or an arm would rest. There were spiderwebs in the corners of the ceiling, and the drapes beside the windows were threadbare and torn. Most of the light bulbs were burned out, the remaining bulbs illuminating the room in a sickly yellow light.

"Sit down," the man said, pointing to a small kitchen table in the center of what appeared to be the living room.

"All right," I said.

I pulled out one of the wooden chairs and sat in it.

"What is it you want?" he said.

I told the man the story of the accident. He stared at me and listened to it all without interrupting. When I was done, he didn't say anything for a few seconds. Then he scratched behind his ear and grunted to himself.

"Looks like you're still pretty banged up."

"It doesn't hurt anymore."

"You want a root beer?"

"Sure. Thank you."

Along one wall was a countertop and sink, stove, and refrigerator. The man wheeled across the floor to the refrigerator. He got out two bottles of Barq's root beer and brought them to the table. He parked across from me, opened both of them with the edge of a pocketknife, and slid one over. I picked it up and took a long swallow and didn't remember anything ever tasting so good.

The man was fidgety. His hands and everything about him seemed to constantly twitch.

"How'd you get here?" he asked.

"I walked."

"From where?"

"Cross City."

"Cross City?"

"Yes, sir."

"That's a long walk."

"Yes, sir. It is."

"What for?"

"I told you. Because I want to find the person who lived here that was supposed to have seen a Bigfoot."

"Okay. Here I am."

I drew a deep breath, relaxed into my chair, and took another swig of root beer.

"I just want to talk to somebody else who's seen one," I continued. "Just to know I'm not losing my mind."

The man took another swallow, set the bottle on the table, and leaned back in his chair.

"You're mighty young for all this."

"I wish I'd never seen it."

"I know how you feel. You can't sleep, can you?"

I shook my head.

"You have nightmares?"

"Yes, sir."

"You think maybe I can fix all this for you?"

"I don't know what to think anymore."

He leaned forward and locked eyes with me. "If it's proof you came looking for, you won't find it here. All I've got is old stories. Stories nobody wants to hear."

"I want to hear them," I said.

9

THE MAN STUDIED ME LIKE HE MIGHT CHANGE HIS MIND ABOUT telling me the stories. But after a moment he sat back in the wheelchair and began talking.

"I saw it sitting out there in my pasture with its legs crossed. Leaning over one of my cows it had ripped apart. It looked up at me, and its eyes were black as caves. It had blood dripping from its mouth. Had teeth like a person. Had a face like a person. Like a caveman or something. But it was covered in hair and must have been ten feet tall. It wasn't scared of me at all."

"What was it?"

"An abomination. Something that's been around a lot longer than us. Inbred and crossbred into all different kinds of things. Part ape, part human, maybe part other stuff."

"How many do you think there are?"

"Hard to say. People see them all over the world."

"I mean around here?"

"There must have been a bigger group at one time. Maybe they migrated down in the fall and went back north in the spring. Now my guess is that there's only a dozen, or less, though I've only ever seen the one."

"The one I saw was headed this way. He was crossing the road in this direction."

"The Refuge is their wintering ground. You used to hear them in the night, starting around this time of year. At first I thought it was coyotes or wildcats. Then I saw that big one out in the pasture. And I remembered how my grandpa told me about swamp apes in the hammock. I was a boy about your age then. I thought he was trying to scare me into staying close. I think he always knew about them."

"Do you still hear them?"

"No. I think they stay deeper in the Refuge now. But they used to come around a lot. I remember one time my grandpa took me out to feed the cows. When we were done, he had me sit on the tailgate of his truck with a sack of sulfur. Had me sprinkle it on the ground while he drove around the outside of the pasture fence. Said it kept out snakes and swamp apes."

"They don't like the way it smells?"

"I don't know. I guess. He never said."

"Can they talk?"

"Not that I've ever heard. But they can do lots of things."

"Like what?"

The man leaned forward and got his root beer and sat back with it. He took another swallow.

"Tell me your name again."

"Adam Parks."

"Travis Stanley," he said. "People just call me Stanley. I'd come over and shake your hand, but as you can see, I don't get around too easy."

"That's fine," I said.

"They never found your parents?"

"No, sir. I'm living with my Uncle John. I guess he's wondering where I am."

"You could call him if I had a phone."

I looked down and shook my head. "He'd just come get me. But I'm not ready to go. I need some more answers about these things."

"I hate to break it to you, but that's the big problem. There's lots of theories and opinions, but no answers."

"I don't understand how people can't know about them."

"The government covers it up. You go public with any convincing evidence, and they'll get rid of it. Then they'll send the military in to try and kill it."

"But there's stuff all over the internet."

"Yeah, in case you haven't noticed, there's stuff about everything all over the internet."

"But there's all the encounter stories and pictures and videos."

"You ever seen a real clear photo or video of a Sasquatch?"

I shook my head.

"That's right. And most people will tell you all those stories of sightings are from wackos or people making them up for attention. And that's what the government wants you to think."

"Why would they cover it up?"

"Some say people would be too scared to go in the woods anymore. Then the national park system would fail, which would hurt the economy. Some say environmental groups would try to protect these things and hurt the logging business. I think some of that might be true, but it doesn't make total sense. These creatures are spotted all over the planet. You can't tell me every government in the world has gotten together and decided to hide these things. No, there's more to it. I think the government's come up against something they don't know how to control. And the last thing a politician wants to admit is he's not in control."

I nodded, taking it all in.

"These creatures can do things that aren't natural."

"Like what?"

Stanley paused while he took another sip of his root beer.

"There's a part of the story I didn't tell that BSO reporter. I didn't think they'd believe me, but now I've read about others that reported the same thing."

"You mean the reports about them coming from UFOs?"

"Naw, I never saw anything like that. I'm talking about infrasound. The thing made me sick."

"Like how?"

"It made me queasy and confused. It can emit something that does it—like a sound frequency we can't hear. Some people think they use it to make pictures blurry. I think that's crap, but I know it made me sick. It was some sort of defense it had."

"Like a dog whistle?"

"Yeah, maybe like that. But it ain't got nothing to do with UFOs and magic and any of that crap. Tigers make infrasound. Other animals can do it. I think these things are flesh and blood. It eats and it bleeds and it dies. But in ways it's far more advanced than we are."

"Do you think they're dangerous?"

"I think they mostly want to be left alone. But yes, if you try to cross one, it's dangerous. They're what you call apex predators. And they eat meat. I've read about them tearing the heads off bull elk. That one I saw tore my cow into pieces like it was no more than a chicken. They're so strong, it's unbelievable."

"You think they'd eat a person?"

"I do. If they're hungry enough. The Nez Perce people claim these things eat their own dead. I believe that. That's why you don't find their bodies."

"Like cannibals?"

"I don't see it that way. Something that big needs a lot of food to survive. I think they do it for practical reasons."

"There's got to be a way to get proof. To let people know. Didn't you try?"

Stanley leaned forward and put his root beer on the table.

"How far down this rabbit hole do you really want to go?"

"I want to know everything," I said.

He studied me for a long, uncomfortable moment.

"If you knew what was good for you," he finally said, "you'd get up from this table and go home to your uncle and convince yourself what you saw was a trick of the mind and I'm just as looney as everybody says I am."

"I don't think I can do that," I said.

"I know you can't."

10

"HOW MUCH DO YOU KNOW ABOUT THE SUWANNEE RIVER?"

"I mean, I've crossed over it a bunch of times. And I've seen it from the bridge. And . . . I guess my parents drowned in it."

"You keep walking down this road and take your first right," Stanley continued. "You'll get to Yellow Jacket Landing, and you'll be looking right at it. Water's black as ink down this way. It's almost impossible to find anything once it sinks. You won't see a darker, more mysterious river in this country. It's like something pulled straight out of the Amazon jungle, surrounded by miles of river swamp and hammock, full of snakes and alligators. You know there's things living out there you can't find anywhere else in the world?"

I shook my head.

"A type of bass, for one," he continued. "They call it the Suwannee bass. And you've got the Suwannee cooter, a turtle. You know about the sturgeon?"

"I've heard about them in school."

"Nobody knows why they come here. Like something left over from the dinosaur age."

I nodded.

"The Indians considered it a sacred, mystical river, fed by hidden crystal clear springs deep in the Refuge. They said if you drank from these springs you would have eternal youth."

"Like what Ponce de León looked for?"

"Exactly. The Fountain of Youth."

"Do you believe it?"

"I think UFOs and magical springs are crap, but that's not my point. Yeah, there's springs out there. There's the ones you know about, Fanning Springs and Manatee Springs and probably a lot more we haven't found. But the Suwannee hammock is so thick and impenetrable, just about anything could be in it. They made it into a refuge because there's no commercial value. It's too wet to build in, too wet to even log timber. It's a place man's not meant to be, period . . . But these creatures, they're so at home in our natural environment—even places like the hammock—it's like *we're* the aliens and they've always been here. They live out there. And I think at one time they hunted this area. Maybe that's when I'd hear them at night. And then they'd go back into the Refuge when they were done. They know nobody's going to follow them into it."

"So you didn't try?"

"Of course I did," he said.

Stanley wheeled back from the table and crossed the floor and pointed up at a bookshelf.

"Grab that photo album for me."

I got up and pulled down the book he was pointing at. It was dusty and covered in dried spiderwebs. I gave it to him and followed him back to the table.

"Pull your chair next to me," he said.

• • •

I don't think he wanted me to see that first page. It had obviously been a while since he'd looked at the pictures, and I think he turned to it by mistake. The photo was of Stanley with a pretty young woman and a girl who appeared to be about six years old. He wasn't in a wheelchair and looked young and strong and happy. They were standing outdoors, in front of a sign that read HUNTSVILLE SPACE AND ROCKET CENTER.

"Was that your family?" I asked.

"Wife and daughter," he mumbled.

"Where are they now?"

"I don't know," he said, like he didn't want to talk about it. He flipped to the center of the album, then quickly flipped a few pages back. The next photo I saw was of Stanley by himself. He was still young, dressed in full camouflage, standing on a green lawn with a deer rifle slung over his shoulder. I thought I recognized a corner of the old barn at the edge of the picture, except the barn looked new and freshly painted.

"She took that," he said. "Before I left."

"Your wife?"

He nodded slowly, like he was thinking more of the photo than what I was saying. "She didn't want to," he continued.

"Why not?"

He didn't answer me.

"Where were you going?" I asked.

He studied the picture another moment. "I was going to find it," he finally said. "And kill it."

11

STANLEY TURNED THE PAGE OF THE PHOTO ALBUM AGAIN, AND
this time I saw several photos of a dark, calm river and a
high wall of lush green trees on the other side. There was
also a picture of him in a small aluminum boat, looking
like he was about to motor out into the water.

"Did she take that one too?"

"Yeah," he said. "I used to keep that jon boat down at
the landing on a little piece of property my dad left me. I
guess it's probably still there, leaning up against the same
tree."

"You went after them in a boat?"

"Yeah. Then I took the camera from her and shoved
off. I was going to document everything and bring back a
dead body and put an end to all of this."

"Did your wife believe you? Did she know about them?"

"She thought I'd lost my mind. That's why I had to go out there. I had to show her."

"She never saw it?"

Stanley shook his head. "No," he said. "And I should have just kept my mouth shut about it . . . But you can't, you know? Not at first."

"I know," I said.

"I mean, you just have to talk to somebody about it."

"How far did you go?"

Stanley took a deep breath and then another sip of his drink. After a moment he continued.

"Eighteen miles downriver is Gopher Creek. That creek is a pathway straight into the deepest part of the Refuge. I knew if I really wanted to find these things, it was my best way in."

On the opposite page was a photo of houseboats tied along the riverbank. I pointed to it. "Where is that?" I asked.

"Fowler's Bluff. About halfway. The only civilization between Yellow Jacket and the Gulf of Mexico. There's not much to it. Just a boat launch and a little store and those houseboats you see."

He turned the page to a picture of a hand holding a compass.

"After Fowler's Bluff you drop off into the biggest part of the Refuge. Nothing but black water and islands and creek mouths. Tall cypress and gum trees. Then there's a big northwest bend in the river. After that Gopher Creek comes in on the left."

He pointed to a picture of an opening in the trees where a small creek entered the river.

"It gets tight in there," he said. "I went as far up it as I could. Until I was dragging the boat through the mud. Then I left it and went looking for high ground. I figured maybe I'd find some sign of them. I could sit there and listen for them. Then I'd know I was in the right place."

"And then you'd wait?"

"That's right. They'd already know I was there. And they'd show themselves when they wanted to."

"And then you'd shoot one?"

Stanley nodded. "You got it."

He flipped the page, and I saw a picture of a small one-man tent and a campfire. There was a clothesline strung between two trees and a shirt and socks hanging on it. He flipped the page again, and I saw a fish cooking on a spit over a campfire. Then he suddenly closed the photo album and put it in his lap.

"So what happened?" I said.

"I couldn't do it, that's what happened."

"Why not?"

"I just couldn't stay out there like that. I had a family back home. It was too dangerous."

"How long were you gone?"

"Three days. It took me that long to realize what I was up against. And I came to see it was impossible. Three days and I was covered with ticks and had been eaten up by yellow flies and mosquitoes. I had snakes crawling in my tent and things creeping around my campsite and howling in the night. I just couldn't do it."

"So you heard them?"

"I don't know what I heard, but it was god-awful."

"So you never saw another one?"

"Let me tell you something. If you want to see a swamp ape or Bigfoot—whatever you want to call it—you've got to be out in the wilderness for weeks. Maybe months. Miles from anything. No fires, no tent, nothing. Until you run out of food and have to live like an animal. Until you're so primitive you dig worms from the ground with your hands and eat them just to go on another day. Then maybe they'll show themselves to you. You understand? A man can't do that."

I nodded.

"Then there's the killing part. Let's say I managed to get far enough out into the Refuge and survive long enough to see one of these things. Let's say I got close enough to take a shot with a high-powered rifle like a .30-06. This is an animal that can weigh a thousand pounds.

Maybe more. I'd have to shoot it in the heart. And let's say I'm lucky and its heart is in the same place as ours. And say I get even luckier and kill it. Then what?"

Stanley paused. I shook my head to show that I didn't have an answer.

"Then you've still got to deal with the other ones. You think they're going to like you shooting one of their family members?"

I shook my head.

"But let's say there's not any more. Say this thing's by itself. Now what? How are you going to drag a thousand pounds of dead weight out of there? You can't leave and come back for it. Alligators and coyotes will eat it. Or maybe *they* eat it."

"But why did you have to kill it?"

"You want proof, you're going to have to bring back a body."

"But maybe just good pictures would do. I mean, if you just had enough good pictures."

"That's been tried, right? The government confiscates any decent proof that ever goes public. The blurry stuff that's left, people just write off as a hoax. No, you're gonna have to have a body. And that's impossible."

"What if there was a way to make it public before the government could get to it?"

"If you can figure a way to do that, then you'll be the first."

Stanley stopped talking and looked at me long and hard. And right off, I couldn't think of a way to solve the problem. After a few seconds I looked over at the window. I hadn't realized how long we'd been talking. The day was getting late, and the sun was already down behind the trees.

"So I guess that's my roundabout way of telling you I don't have the answers," he said. "Nobody does. Nobody ever will."

I looked up at him.

"Do you mind if I spend the night here?"

"I suppose it's too late to start back. You're welcome to sleep in the extra bedroom. Been a while since anybody's stayed in there, but it should be okay."

"Thanks," I said.

"I've got some beef stew. You hungry?"

"Yes, sir. Thank you."

Stanley wheeled into the kitchen and got a pot of what I assumed was the stew out of the refrigerator and set it on the stove. He reached up and turned the knob for the gas, and I saw the flames leap up under the pot and begin heating it.

"How do you get groceries?" I asked.

Stanley spun around in the chair and went back to the refrigerator.

"Another root beer?" he said.

"Sure," I said.

He pulled out another Barq's and stuck it between his legs. Then he brought out a bottle of Old Forester. He went to the sink and got a glass and poured it half full of the whiskey, set the bottle on the counter, and came back to the table.

"Buddy of mine stops by here once a week. Brings me stuff," he said.

He opened the Barq's and passed it to me. "You don't ever leave?" I asked.

"I go to the doctor every now and then. My buddy drives me into town."

"What happened?" I asked. "I mean, I saw the pictures. You weren't always in a wheelchair."

Stanley raised the glass with shaking hands. He took a long swallow of the whiskey and winced and wheezed and set the glass down on the table. He studied me for a moment, like he was thinking about how to answer.

"I shot myself," he said.

Suddenly, I was sorry I'd asked.

12

I DIDN'T KNOW IF STANLEY WAS TALKING ABOUT AN ACCIDENT or if he'd tried to kill himself. He didn't seem to want to explain, and I wasn't about to ask. So we both sat there in silence, him drinking his whiskey and me sipping on the Barq's. An uncomfortable feeling hung over me. And I was suddenly uneasy about being there.

Finally he spoke. "Why don't you go down that hall to the last room on the left? See if it suits you."

"Okay," I said.

I got up, glad to get away from the heavy silence. I walked down the hall until I came to the last door. It was closed. I turned the knob and gently pushed. The door swung open on creaky hinges, and what I saw before me, in the pale dusky light through the windows, was shocking. It was a young girl's bedroom, everything arranged like she was coming home at any moment. Except a musty smell of entombment hung in the air like no one had been inside the room in years.

I stepped through the door and looked around. There was a small bed with a white chenille cover and canary yellow pillows and stuffed animals. Beside it was a bookcase with dolls and picture books. There was a dresser with a photo of the girl I'd seen in Stanley's album. The room would have been full of color had it not been dulled by a light coating of dust. Then I began to notice the same spiderwebs in the corners of the ceiling. On the floor, at the base of the windows, were hundreds of dead wasps. I turned and walked out, suddenly desperate to think of an excuse to tell Stanley why I couldn't stay.

When I came to the living room again, he was at the table with two steaming bowls of stew, spoons, and napkins. He had refilled his whiskey glass, and there was a cup of ice water next to my bowl.

"Everything all right in there?" he asked.

I nodded. "Yeah," I said.

"Have a seat. Eat it while it's hot."

I sat down and studied the stew. It looked fine, and I was hungry, but now I was nervous about everything. I was afraid of what was in the stew.

"It was your daughter's room," I said.

Stanley ate, chewing and staring at his bowl. "That's right," he said.

I grabbed my spoon and scooped a small sample of the stew and looked at it. I couldn't bring myself to eat it. And then I had to know.

"What happened to her?" I said.

Stanley looked up at me and stopped chewing. After a second he set his spoon down and reached over and got the whiskey and kept his eyes on me while he took a big swallow. He wheezed and coughed and set the glass down again, then leaned back in his wheelchair.

"Swamp apes," he said.

My heart was thudding. *Was he saying the creatures had taken her? Could that be true?*

"Swamp apes," he said again. "They get a piece of your soul. Something you can't ever get back. You understand?"

I didn't understand what he was saying, but I nodded as if I did.

"What drives you mad isn't seeing them. It's not having the answers. Not a night goes by I don't dream about those things. The man you saw in those photos was a different person. I don't even remember what he was like. I know he didn't know a damn thing about what was really out in this world."

Stanley leaned forward and kept his eyes locked on me.

"They took a piece of your soul, didn't they?" he said.

I knew the encounter had changed me, and now I understood what Stanley was getting at, but it wasn't a conversation I wanted to have. I looked down at my bowl and didn't respond.

"I want to kill every last one of them for what they did to me," he grumbled. "But it won't help. It won't bring my wife back. It won't bring back my little girl."

"You don't have to tell me about it," I said quietly.

"There's nothing to tell. They left me. Not long after I came back from the woods. I tried to get it all out of my head, but I couldn't. Swamp apes . . . How do you just forget seeing something like that? So she said she couldn't live here anymore. Packed up my daughter and took her away."

I drew a deep breath. I looked up at him.

"I'm sorry?" I said.

Stanley leaned back again. "My daughter's in Orlando, last I heard. That was ten years ago. I don't know where my wife is."

I nodded and took a bite of the stew. I was so distracted, I forgot to worry about it. Then all of a sudden I was chewing the meat. It wasn't bad, but it didn't seem to have any taste.

Stanley grabbed the glass, wheeled his chair around, and started for the kitchen again.

"You don't want to hear all this," he said over his shoulder.

"It's okay," I said, immediately regretting my words.

He poured the glass full this time and took a big swig from the bottle while he was facing the sink. He coughed and wiped his mouth with the back of his hand and put the bottle back on the counter.

"What can you believe in after you see something like that?" he said.

"I don't know," I said.

"Who can you trust?"

I didn't answer. He took a swallow from the glass and turned to face me.

"How do you even have religion after that?"

"Maybe I should go home," I said. "I'm starting to feel bad about my uncle worrying."

"I'm responsible for you now. You're staying here until tomorrow. You can head back first thing in the morning."

"I think I'll be fine. I walked here in the dark."

He took another swallow and wheeled toward me.

"You can't go out there," he said. "You're staying here. Come on."

He wheeled past me to the front door and opened it and rolled onto the porch. It was dark now, and I heard the cheeping of tree frogs and insects.

"Come out here," he said over his shoulder.

I got up slowly, planning to make a run for it, then something he said distracted me.

"God, I'm lonely," he said into the darkness.

And in that moment I felt sorry for him, and I thought maybe I could just talk to him and make him feel better. Make both of us feel better.

I came up behind him. "Maybe your wife was just scared of them coming around. Maybe you could go find her."

"I'm not leaving here. This is my home. She knows that. My grandpa built this place. Cleared that back pasture with a mule."

"Maybe it's not worth it," I said.

Stanley took another swallow of whiskey and lowered the glass. "Look out there," he said.

I gazed into the darkness. I couldn't see anything but moths fluttering around the porch light.

"Swamp apes," he said.

"What?"

"I come out here every night. They're gonna be back one of these days. And I'm gonna get mine. I'm gonna lay it out right on this lawn. And I'm gonna load that thing up in a FedEx van and ship it to Orlando or wherever the hell she is. They can dump it on her living room floor."

In that moment I decided that Stanley was crazy. He didn't care about his family at all. All he cared about, all he lived for, was revenge. Revenge on the creatures. Revenge on anyone who doubted him, starting with his wife. Revenge he'd never get.

"I need you to find me a gun," he said. "They took my guns. They took everything."

I thought about the pack, still sitting next to the table. I began to back away from him. Suddenly he spun in the chair and looked at me, and I froze. His eyes were bloodshot and his teeth were clenched.

"Find me a gun," he said.

13

I FELT MY PULSE POUNDING IN MY EARS.

"What do you mean?"

"I'll pay you. Go find me a gun."

"Where?"

"Anywhere. Does your uncle have one? I'll buy it from him."

I shook my head. "He doesn't have one," I lied.

He wheeled closer to me and leaned in. "We'll do this together," he whispered. "You and me. I know how to find them. We'll bring one out of there."

I stepped back. "You already said it was impossible."

He closed the distance. "I've got it figured out," he continued. "Once we kill it, we cut it into five pieces. The head, two hands, and two feet. We mail them to five different news stations. How's the government going to get ahead of that?"

"I don't want to kill one," I said.

"There's no other way. You've got to have a body."

"But . . . you can't walk," I said.

"I know I can't walk!" he suddenly yelled. "I can't do a thing but sit here and rot while those hellish freaks of nature swing from the trees and laugh at us all!"

I took another step back.

"They're flesh and blood," he said.

"I'm really tired," I said.

"There's no magic out there. There's no UFOs. It's just an abomination!"

I turned slowly and started for the table.

"I want my guns back," he said.

I got to my pack and picked it up and slung it over my shoulder. I heard the wheels of his chair squeaking as he came up behind me. I spun around, and he wasn't even six inches from me.

"If I really wanted to kill myself, I would have done it right the first time," he said.

I sidestepped and bolted for the door. I leapt off the porch, clearing the front steps and stumbling on the lawn. I regained my footing and fled into the night.

• • •

I came to the end of Stanley's driveway and stopped running and turned to look back at the farmhouse. The door was still wide open, and I saw him sitting in his wheelchair in the middle of the floor, moths flitting around his head, his eyes staring in my direction. I knew he couldn't see or follow me, but the sight of him was creepy, and I didn't want to be anywhere near him. I repositioned the pack on my shoulder and started toward the highway. I went about fifty yards before I stepped off onto the roadside and sat down to catch my breath and collect myself.

• • •

I've spent a lot of time thinking about not just what happened but how it came to happen. Because there are certain events that, had they gone another way, would have led to a completely different outcome. My encounter with Stanley was certainly one of them.

Much of what he'd said I didn't want to think about. But there was one thing that I couldn't get out of my head:

What drives you mad isn't seeing them. It's not having the answers.

Finding Stanley was supposed to be about getting questions answered to make sure I wasn't crazy. Nothing more. Now I knew there were no answers. And I'd seen firsthand what happened to people like me that didn't get them. Maybe I wasn't crazy yet, but like Stanley, I could see myself eventually losing my mind.

In that moment, sitting on the edge of the roadside, I began to consider going after the creatures myself. I'd already seen one walking this way, and Stanley had pretty much given me directions to where it was going. It seemed that all it was going to take to find them was a boat journey and some camping. Stanley already had a boat at the landing he wasn't even using. And surely the camping part of it couldn't be as bad as he'd said. Maybe he'd just been lonely. I was already lonely, and it didn't seem like I could get any lonelier. Maybe he'd just gone at the wrong time of year when it was too hot, the bugs too bad, and the snakes too active. The weather was cool now, the yellow flies gone, and the snakes sluggish.

I don't remember it even crossing my mind how foolish all this really was. The fact is, I'd come to a dead end, and there didn't seem to be another choice. And so I was doing my best to talk myself into it all, ignoring the true dangers I was likely to face. So much of this journey would come to that. Time and time again I found myself facing paths that led only in one direction.

So I convinced myself to go. Which left just one thing: bringing back the evidence.

Despite all the technical problems of shooting a

Bigfoot, I didn't think I could morally bring myself to do it. The things seemed so close to human. Just the thought of killing one felt like murder.

I remembered the camera, took off my pack, and dug inside until I felt it. Thirty-two pictures left. It seemed so simple. If I could get good enough pictures and email them to everyone I knew, even to people I didn't know, how could they ever track them all down?

I just have to get good pictures, I thought.

I had to journey into the Refuge, find the creatures, and take good pictures. I was convinced it was the only way to save myself from becoming like Stanley.

Now comes the *what happened* part of the story. And it's the part you probably won't believe.

14

I NEEDED A TENT, SLEEPING BAG, MORE FOOD, AND A WAY TO
make fire. But there were no stores nearby, and even had
there been, I had only twelve dollars. I could certainly get all
of these supplies if I went back home, but that brought about
a whole new set of complications involving Uncle John.

I walked back to the end of Stanley's driveway and
studied the house. He was gone from the porch, but the
front door stayed open and the lights were still on. I didn't
want to get into a conversation about the guns, but I
needed to ask him for supplies. I decided to spend the
night outside and talk to him in the morning after he'd
had time to sleep off the whiskey. I figured he'd understand what I needed to do and give me a tent and blankets
and canned food and a box of matches.

I looked over at the old barn. It would certainly be more comfortable to sleep with a roof over my head. I crept through the yard, keeping my eyes on the house. I didn't want him to know I was there. I imagined him screaming at me from the porch all night, begging for his guns and threatening the swamp apes. When I came to the barn, I pulled on the door and it swung open on rusty hinges that popped and creaked. I looked at the house again. Still no Stanley. I pulled the penlight out of my pocket, clicked it on, and stepped inside.

The air smelled of decayed wood and dirt. I passed the light around the barn and saw a workbench to my right with a scattering of old tools and oil cans and jars of nuts and bolts. In front of me, toward the back, the fallen-in roof lay in a mess of rotten beams and sheet tin with the night sky visible above it. To my left I saw what looked like two stables. Hanging on nails were mildewed leather bridles and miscellaneous horse tack. Draped over a railing was a stack of saddle blankets. Overhead were the remains of the hayloft.

I walked over to the workbench. There was a shelf above it with what looked like a tackle box. I pulled it down, opened it, and picked through a tangle of old corks, fishing lures, hooks, and lead sinkers.

I can use this, I thought.

I closed the tackle box and shined my light under the workbench and down it to my left. I saw what appeared to be a metal shipping container about the size of the chest I took to church camp. I walked to it and opened the lid. I couldn't believe what I was looking at. It was full of what appeared to be dehydrated food rations. I pulled out a bag of dried apples and looked at the label. The expiration date was nearly three years past. I dropped it and grabbed a can of something else. PINTO BEANS, it read. 2 LBS. EXPIRATION DATE 2035. I grabbed three cans of the beans and set them aside. Then I dug again, finding more dried fruit, canned meats and vegetables, and a stack of fifteen military MREs. All of these were expired. But I set aside ten boxes of pasta and powdered cheese. Four cans of dehydrated carrots. These were okay.

I looked over my shoulder at the saddle blankets. Back at the tackle box.

I've got everything I need here! I don't have to wait on Stanley at all! I've got food, blankets to stay warm, equipment to catch fish. I can use my poncho for a lean-to instead of a tent . . . Matches. I need matches.

I began searching the workbench and shelves above it, looking for a box of matches. A moment later I found something even better—a grill lighter. I clicked it and it still worked.

And now I've got a way to make fire!

I spread one of the saddle blankets on the dirt floor and began piling my supplies onto it. The tackle box, grill lighter, mac and cheese, pinto beans, carrots, and salt. The food wasn't going to make an ideal meal, but it was enough to keep me from going hungry. For a brief moment I considered that I had nothing to cook in, then reasoned I could empty one of the cans and use it for a pot.

Fork? Spoon? I can use my pocket knife for a fork. But I need a spoon. And something to pick up the pot with.

I grabbed a pair of pliers off the workbench and tossed them onto the blanket. I searched only a moment more before I found a measuring spoon next to a jar of what looked like gunpowder. It would certainly do to stir and eat with.

I tossed the spoon onto the blanket, gathered the four corners together, and tied them with a short piece of baling wire. Then I found an old broom, broke off the end, and shoved the stick under the wire. I lifted it all and slung it over my shoulder like I'd seen hoboes do in movies.

I was so excited about my finds I forgot about being tired and couldn't think of any reason not to set out immediately.

I need to go and look for Stanley's boat and get on the river. I need to travel at night so I'm not stopped by anyone.

I grabbed my backpack and started for the door.

15

AT NINE O'CLOCK THAT NIGHT, I SET OUT FOR THE RIVER
landing, wearing the backpack and toting the bundle of
camping supplies over my shoulder. The woods on either
side of the road were dark and quiet except for the cheeping of crickets. I soon came to an intersection and turned
right. I didn't walk far before I saw a light glowing through
the trees and heard the river, softly licking and slurping
through the hammock. Then I began to hear loud smacking noises like someone hitting the water with a board. I
couldn't imagine what it could be making such a sound.

The road ended and I wasn't prepared for the enormity
of what I saw before me, reflecting the faint moonlight
like a black mirror, six hundred feet wide, deep and heavy-
looking, oozing past like something alive. In every

direction the hammock cheeped and pulsed against it, like this river was the mother of all things. Every minute or so another smacking sound echoed across the water like gunshots. Then it occurred to me that I'd heard beavers slap their tails and make a similar noise. And I decided it had to be beavers making such a racket.

To my left was the light I'd seen earlier through the trees, a tall utility pole that hummed and cast a faint yellow glow over a boat dock. To my right was a wooded lot I guessed was Stanley's. I made my way down the riverbank under the shadows of giant tupelo gum and cypress. I set the bundle of supplies on the ground and searched for the boat with my penlight. I soon found what had to be the old aluminum jon, leaning against a tree, overgrown with vines and briars. There was no motor on it, but I figured I could find a board to use as a paddle. I saw a rusty chain running through the bow eye and ran my hand along it until I felt a padlock. I looked around, scanning the area for the boat anchor, which I found lying on the ground. I picked it up and banged the lock until it opened. Then I pulled the chain off, the clacking sound seeming to echo clear across the river.

I tore the jon away from the overgrowth and rolled it over. Beneath was an aluminum paddle and life jacket. The paddle still seemed to be in good enough shape. The life jacket was ripped and rotten, but the foam core still seemed intact. It would have to do. I hung the life jacket around my neck and put the backpack and paddle in the center of the boat where the seat was. Then I retrieved the supply bundle and stowed it in the rear. Finally I grabbed the handle on the front of the jon and pulled it all to the river's edge.

I stood back and looked at the powerful water. I tried to think of anything I was forgetting, but really, I knew I was only giving myself a last chance to turn back.

● ● ●

I pushed off the bank and began paddling toward the middle of the river. I'd been in motorboats a few times. I'd paddled rafts and canoes at church camp. It hadn't crossed my mind just how different this would be. The jon was clumsy and hard to steer. As the strong current gripped the hull and swept me along, I was alarmed to find I wasn't in control at all. I looked over my shoulder and saw the utility light at the dock falling farther behind and stopped paddling, paralyzed with the fear I'd made a fatal mistake. I wanted to cry out for help, but even my voice seemed frozen. I tried to paddle backward, but my strokes were useless. I looked ahead again, searching the darkness, desperately trying to get some idea of where I was in the river. The water was so black that the shadowy border of trees blended into the edges of it, and it was impossible to discern the riverbank. I felt like I was being swept through a deep black canyon. Suddenly an enormous fish erupted from the water not ten yards from me. I couldn't see it clearly, but it must have been five feet long and weighed eighty pounds. It sailed several feet into the air and smacked down again, making that same noise I'd been hearing. I knew immediately I'd seen my first sturgeon up close. Too close. I lowered the paddle and felt the boat rocking from the disturbance. I recalled the stories of people being killed by these giants slamming into them, and I was flooded with more fear. Then the boat bumped into something, and I was thrown forward onto the floor. I gripped the paddle and lay there, terrified, feeling the boat swing around a log. With my ear pressed to the thin aluminum, I heard the river licking and tapping against the metal. I pulled the paddle closer and balled up helplessly.

It couldn't have been more than twenty minutes before I heard a scraping sound against the jon and a large cypress bough swept over me. Then the boat swung around and hung there. I lay still for a moment, staring up into the tree. Because the branch came from my left, I reasoned I'd either come up against the other side of the river or an island. But I was relieved to be stopped, even just to know it was possible to reach land again. At the same time I knew if I wanted to get out and quit, I had no idea where I was and if it was possible to walk to civilization from this place.

After a moment my breathing slowed and I grew calmer. I remembered I'd only heard of sturgeon killing people in speeding motorboats. And despite a few obstacles and my fears, I'd safely crossed the river in the jon. Surely I could drift down it. And I could get out at the place Stanley called Fowler's Bluff if I needed to.

I pushed myself from under the limb and sat up and paddled toward the middle of the river again. This time, when I felt the current take hold, I didn't fight it. I hung the paddle over the side and used it like a rudder. I looked up at the sky and used the gap of light to get a sense of where the channel was. The technique wasn't very accurate, but it was enough to keep the boat far enough from the riverbank so I wasn't swept under more limbs.

After a few minutes I was no longer startled by every explosion of the sturgeon. I settled into my new routine and let the river take me gently along under the stars and through the darkness.

16

MY CONFIDENCE GREW AS I DRIFTED FARTHER DOWNRIVER.
The jon was clumsy, but as long as I didn't count on any
fast maneuvers, I could use the paddle to move in the
direction I wanted. The echoing smacks of the sturgeon
never let up, like there must have been thousands of them
racing the black depths. But I gradually realized they
tended to stay in the middle of the straightaways and the
outside edges of the turns, preferring the swiftest, deepest
parts of the channel. By aligning the jon a little off-center
and steering the inside of the river bends, I was able to
avoid most of their traffic. It was only when the river
changed direction, and I had to recross to reach the slack
water inside the bend, that I became tense and felt my
adrenaline spike. I gripped the paddle tightly, imagining I
was drifting over a minefield.

On a long, straight part of the river, I had time to get out my penlight and pass it over the water. The weak beam didn't travel far, but enough to see something that sent fear coursing through me. The reflective orange eyes of alligators floated quietly in all directions. As the jon approached, they submerged, but I knew they were still down there waiting for the boat to glide over. And when I turned and shined the light behind me, they were there again.

For a while I waved the light from side to side, trying to spot all the alligators, like it would somehow fend them off. But gradually I realized the uselessness of my efforts. And I reminded myself what it was I had come to do and that I was safe in the boat. And that I needed to conserve the penlight batteries. So I shut off the light and scooted more to the center of the seat and kept my hands away from the water.

• • •

It was close to two o'clock in the morning when I saw a scattering of lights along the left riverbank. Even with the fast-moving current, it surprised me that I would have arrived at Fowler's Bluff so soon. According to Stanley it was the only landmark between Yellow Jacket and the Gulf of Mexico. And my last chance to stop if I wanted to turn back.

As I came closer I saw several houseboats and a store and boat ramp. Behind the store were a few houses and street lights. I thought of the people inside, sleeping in comfortable beds. These people were different than me now. They didn't have images of giant ape-men burned into their memories. They could sleep at night, believing the world was only what they'd been taught. I slipped quietly past it all, my mind already made up. I wasn't stopping.

I left Fowler's Bluff behind and slipped into the dark canyon once again. By Stanley's reckoning, I'd traveled close to nine miles and was halfway to Gopher Creek. I'd been on the river about three hours and estimated I'd come to the northwest bend at about five o'clock that morning. Then a worrisome thought came over me. It was probably going to be dark when I reached the bend. And then it was going to be almost impossible to spot the entrance to the creek.

I contemplated stopping once I reached the bend, tying up along the riverbank, and sleeping until first light. The only problem I foresaw was encountering fishermen on the river at daybreak. Uncle John surely had the police looking for me by now, and I didn't need anyone asking me questions. But if I missed the creek, there was no way I could paddle upstream against the current. I finally decided to stop before Gopher Creek and take my chances in the morning.

• • •

After nearly three hours the gap in the trees made an obvious turn to my right. I switched on my penlight and looked at the compass on my knife and verified the northwest heading. There were still a couple of hours left until daylight, so I knew I had to stop and wait.

As I rounded the bend, I had to cross the river only once more. Then I would be in the slack water. I could tie up against the riverbank there and wait until sunrise.

I took a stroke with the paddle and thrust the jon toward the opposite side. As I felt the current take hold, I lowered the blade behind me and began to steer across, just like I'd already done at least ten times that night. But for some reason I was more nervous than ever. As I angled closer to the middle, it seemed I could feel the thrum of the giants racing beneath me. It was like I knew what was coming. Or that my luck had run out. Or maybe through my concentration against such a disaster, I willed it to happen.

The enormous fish erupted soundlessly from the water and rose before me, a wall of hard, glimmering scales. It seemed to hang six feet overhead for an impossible amount of time, its powerful tail whipping at the air while it gradually twisted onto its side. I gazed up at a glassy black eye that stared back at me with no emotion. And then, slowly, the ancient creature fell toward me. The full weight of it crashed onto the right gunnel, and it rolled into the boat. The jon tilted onto its side and threw me toward the water. As I clung to the seat, trying not to go over, the sturgeon beat on the aluminum with its armored tail like someone hitting a steel barrel with a sledgehammer. Then I heard the sucking sound of the river pouring into the boat and felt it soaking my jeans. I threw my hands into the air, grasping for the left gunnel above me, but the cold water was already sliding over my waist. Within seconds the boat and fish were gone into the depths below.

17

I FLOATED IN MY LIFE VEST, SLAPPING AT THE SURFACE, TRYING to grasp something—anything. I saw my backpack to my left and grabbed it. Then I felt the paddle and pulled it to me. I looked around for anything else, but there was nothing. The food and supplies I'd stored had sunk or floated away into the darkness. I suddenly felt the turbulence of something jet past my feet, and I thought about the sturgeon racing beneath me. Then I thought about the alligator eyes I'd seen that night. I let go of the paddle, put an arm through one side of the pack, and began to swim for my life.

It was too dark to tell where the riverbank was, but I swam and thrashed across the current with all my strength, aiming for the silhouette of the tree line. I expected to get rammed by a sturgeon or pulled under in the jaws of an alligator. The thought of my feet touching anything sent white-hot fear racing through me.

Go! my head screamed. *Go!*

I thrust my arms ahead and plowed forward. Eventually I felt the current release me, and I breast-stroked into the slack water. After a moment I sensed the darkness getting even darker. Then I was startled to feel something scrape my cap. At first I thought it was a snake, then realized I was swimming under overhanging limbs. I expected to feel solid ground underfoot, but when I kicked down there was nothing but liquid space. This confused me and caused me to panic even more. I flailed my arms until I felt a tree and pulled myself to it. I scraped my feet along its trunk but found nothing to stand on. Finally I hugged it and pressed my cheek against the bark. I tried to cry but nothing came out except coughing.

I rested for only a moment before the fear of alligators and snakes was overwhelming. As tired as I was, I took off my cap and stuffed it down my shirt. Then I let go of the tree and kept swimming deeper into the flooded timber. Limbs slapped me and tore at my head and face, but I plowed through them until my feet pressed into soft mud. I stood up in waist-deep water and fell and stood again and then stumbled forward.

I must have waded a hundred yards into the river bottom before the water was below my knees and the ground was firmer. I began tripping my way through cypress knees and rotten logs until I eventually trudged up onto muddy ground. I collapsed, backed against a tree, clasped my knees close to me, and shivered.

I stared wide-eyed into the darkness, listening to my heavy breathing and chattering teeth. Then the swamp sounds slowly pressed in on me. Frogs and crickets and cicadas. A distant owl. Something splashing out in the water behind me.

I'd always been comforted by the fact that I could make it back to civilization if I really wanted to. That I could give up. Stanley had said there was no other place to stop until you reached the Gulf, but it would have been easy to run across a fisherman. And maybe I could have paddled to shore somewhere and walked to the nearest house or town. But I no longer had those options. Now, I was truly stranded. Nobody would ever find me in this place. And there was no way to get to the river for help without swimming and hanging onto a tree among the snakes and alligators.

I have this trick I play in my head when I'm worried. I try to think of the worst possible thing that can happen and compare that to my own situation. Then I try to diminish the problem enough to feel better about it.

At least I'm still alive, I thought.

I'd never compared myself to being dead before, but it was really the only thing I could think of. The only thing worse than the situation I faced.

I'm going to have to walk out of here. I'll have to find a way out on foot.

I thought about what I'd already seen of the hammock around me. The horror of having to trudge through it overtook me. My fear was so great that I couldn't even process it. If you'd asked me then to choose between coming face-to-face with Bigfoot and walking miles through the Suwannee river bottom I would have chosen Bigfoot without hesitation.

• • •

I remained backed against the cypress tree, quiet and trembling and terrified. I didn't look at my watch, but it seemed like I wasn't there long before the frogs and insects grew silent and the hammock began to purple with daybreak. And as the landscape revealed itself before me, I couldn't have imagined a bleaker sight. Nothing but black mud and rotten logs and cypress knees under a tall canopy of hardwoods for as far as I could see. The place looked dead. I heard no birds or squirrels or any other animal sound usually associated with dawn. I stood slowly and looked out over the dark water and trees I swam through to get here. I knew the river was somewhere in that direction, but I couldn't see it at all. I was so far into the timber that I couldn't even hear a passing boat.

I leaned over and picked up the L.L.Bean backpack. *At least I still have this*, I thought. *I have a poncho and what's left of my snacks. And a change of clothes that will eventually dry out.*

I felt my pocket. *And the pocketknife and penlight.*

It's not much, but it's something.

I had to start moving as soon as possible. Every minute I spent in that soupy wasteland brought me one minute closer to getting eaten by an alligator, being poisoned by a cottonmouth, or starving. I pulled the wet cap out of my shirt and slid it on. Then I slung the pack over my shoulder and started walking away from the river, deeper into the hammock.

18

THE RIVER BOTTOM WAS A LANDSCAPE FROM THE AGE OF THE
dinosaurs, home to nothing but reptiles, amphibians, and
arachnids. I made my way under a shadowy forest canopy
of tupelo gum and cypress, waving away spiderwebs, tripping through cypress knees, and climbing over giant
decaying logs. In some places the mud was thin and watery
with an oily rainbow look to it. I stepped around these
places, thinking of quicksand, all the while watching for
snakes and other unknowns lying in wait.

The first animal I encountered was a loggerhead sea
turtle the size of a trash can lid. I came around a tree to
find myself face-to-face with him, hissing and snapping at
me. I quickly retreated and gave him a wide berth.

After about an hour I came to a narrow creek choked

with duckweed and water lettuce. I stopped and studied it, wary of alligators lurking nearby. I didn't see any but decided to keep my distance from the bank just in case.

I knew the river flowed generally southwest, and I assumed most of the tributaries would come in at right angles, draining the distant uplands. If I was right about that, I figured following the creek would take me somewhere to the southeast, where I'd eventually find higher ground. I didn't know if this was Gopher Creek or some other slough I'd stumbled across. Whatever it was, it was impossible for a boat to get into.

I turned right and began following the watercourse upstream. A half hour later I came to more flooded timber, except this time it was so thick with ferns and briars and underbrush that I didn't see a way through. I was either going to have to walk around it or wade out into the creek and travel up the shallows. It made my heart race just thinking about getting into the water again. Even though I'd yet to see an alligator or a snake that day, I knew they were out there. But heading off in the wrong direction and spending no telling how long trudging miles through the wetland muck seemed even more dangerous. I couldn't survive long in this place. I had no choice. Getting into the water again was my shortest and easiest route to higher ground.

The pack was still wet, but I didn't want to get it any wetter. I hoisted it higher on my shoulders and stepped down into the creek. I pushed my way through the floating vegetation that smelled like broccoli and onions. When I was a few yards from the bank, the canopy opened overhead and sunlight fell over me, warm and welcomed. I continued to the center, relieved to find the channel was no more than waist deep. Then I started upstream, pushing through the water lettuce and stepping softly through the gooey mud.

I must have traveled a quarter mile in this way, the creek gradually narrowing and the aquatic plants thinning. The sky began to cloud over, but the sun still warmed me in brief intervals. And any sunlight was better than the cool dark shade of the river bottom.

The creek was no more than ten feet across when the tree limbs closed overhead and the sunlight was filtered away again. The surface was now clear of all floating vegetation, and the underbrush along the bank had thinned. I stopped and peered deep into the shadowy interior of the swamp. Except for the flash of an occasional yellow or red bird, there seemed to be no color but shades of brown and dirty green. Tall reeds and palmetto and leafy ferns. Then I saw my first cottonmouth, thick as my arm, brown as the mud, oozing through the cypress knees. But my fear had already accounted for these things, and I only studied the snake curiously, convinced that wading the creek had been the safest course after all.

I continued on, and the creek became as shallow and clear as an aquarium. The channel was only a couple of feet wide, bordered with reeds and thin swamp grass hiding glassy minnows and small green and brown water snakes. I stopped and knelt and gazed at my reflection in the water. My face looked a mess. The tree limbs from the night before had left a dozen or more thin cuts. Fortunately they had not reopened the older cuts from the car wreck. These wounds still stood as swollen pink lines with tracks of black sutures. I put my hand to the scar on my cheek and tugged gently at the stitches. The pain made me wince, and I decided to leave them alone for a few more days.

Raindrops began to spot the water around me. Then I heard the distant rumble of thunder. I looked up but saw only leaves and branches overhead. I knew I needed to press on and find high ground and make shelter.

I ducked and splashed up the clear creek. I watched for cottonmouths, but it was hard to see anything. At times the brush was so tight around me it felt like I was walking through a culvert pipe. The sky continued to rumble, and it seemed I could hear the rain hitting the canopy far overhead. In the tunnel the few raindrops I saw dripped from the leaves overhead and twitched the fragile ferns alongside me.

Moving with my head down most of the time, I noticed the creek bottom gradually changing from the muddy silt to white polished gravel. A different type of grass grew here that was flat-topped and thick and broad-stemmed. The water seemed to be getting colder and clearer and cleaner, as if the grass and gravel were filtering it. Occasionally I saw cabbage palms and oaks and sweet-gum, a sign that I was moving out of the river bottom and into the upland hammock.

• • •

It was close to noon when the tunnel suddenly opened into a small clearing. I was shocked to see a jade-blue spring about twenty feet wide and forty feet long, surrounded by a perimeter of shallow, grassy marsh. The creek source bubbled from the center of what looked like a bottomless cave of white limestone.

I approached the spring and stared down into it. Suspended in its depths were all sizes of alligator gar, another long-snouted, primitive-looking fish. I was so amazed it took me a moment to realize how hard the rain was coming down. I backed away from the pool and ducked into the tunnel again. I dug the poncho out of my backpack, tore it open, and pulled it over me. Then I walked up to a small ledge just above the limestone and sat under a cabbage palm.

As I watched the rain falling over the spring, I thought about Dad. I remembered us walking through the forest and him telling me about cabbage palms and how their fronds were dense enough to make a good temporary shelter during a storm. It all seemed so long ago. Like maybe it had never even been real. And I could see myself walking beside him and listening and not really wanting to know about trees and plants, only wanting to shoot the gun. It was hard to think of that boy as me. It was like somebody I didn't know anymore.

I hugged my knees close and pulled my cap brim low over my face. Then I put my forehead down, closed my eyes, and slept.

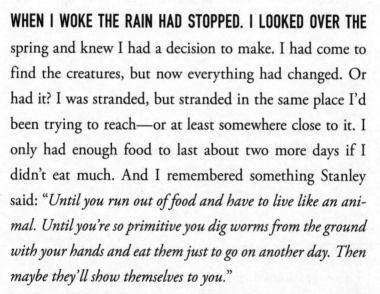

19

WHEN I WOKE THE RAIN HAD STOPPED. I LOOKED OVER THE spring and knew I had a decision to make. I had come to find the creatures, but now everything had changed. Or had it? I was stranded, but stranded in the same place I'd been trying to reach—or at least somewhere close to it. I only had enough food to last about two more days if I didn't eat much. And I remembered something Stanley said: *"Until you run out of food and have to live like an animal. Until you're so primitive you dig worms from the ground with your hands and eat them just to go on another day. Then maybe they'll show themselves to you."*

But Stanley was crazy. Were these things worth dying for? Nobody said anything about having to die for them.

My thoughts kept going in circles, and, despite how I'd arrived, I was soon right back where I started.

I've got no life back home. My parents are missing, probably dead. People think I'm crazy. There's only one way out of this. Get proof these creatures exist. Then you can worry about living.

I stood and began pulling my clothes out of the backpack and spreading them on limbs to dry. Then I set about making camp beneath an oak tree just above the ledge. The slope of its trunk created enough high ground for me to get out of the mud, and the thought of having the tree at my back gave me comfort. I stabbed some sticks into the dirt for uprights and ran more sticks over them to create support for my roof. Then I draped the poncho over it and cut a few palmetto fronds for a floor.

It was late afternoon when I sat under the shelter and ate one of the few packages of peanut butter crackers I had left.

• • •

As the sun slipped low in the trees, I watched the spring. There was something hypnotic about the way the water boiled and rolled and trickled gently into the creek. When darkness fell the air grew chilly, and I began to shiver. I got my jacket and lay down and pulled it over me. Soon it was so dark I couldn't see my hand in front of my face.

It's one thing to walk alone on a highway at night or paddle a boat down a river. There's usually at least a little skylight, and the space around you gives you a sense of safety. You can see things coming. You can imagine an escape. It's another thing entirely to be curled up in a ball with a cheeping, pulsing, dark swamp pressing in on you from all sides. The fear smothers you. It's so dark an animal could have its snout inches from your face and you'd never know it until you felt the breath of the thing on your cheeks.

I heard noises on all sides of me: owls, frogs, whip-poor-wills, whistles and screeches, scratching and thumping. Never had I felt so strongly that I was somewhere I wasn't meant to be. I was as out of place as a deer crouched in a city alley. Maybe I was hidden for now, but it was only a matter of time before I was discovered. And then I was at the mercy of the things living here. I wanted to cry out, but I knew there was no one for miles. And just the thought of my voice echoing through the night terrified me. The thought of shining the penlight terrified me. But the thought of being alone, so absolutely alone in the world, was enough to make me feel like I was going insane.

• • •

I passed out some time that night, mentally and physically exhausted. When I opened my eyes, I saw leaves before me, dappled in soothing sunlight. I heard the trickle of the spring and squirrels fussing and birds calling from deep in the jungle weave of hammock. Then the entire memory of my perilous situation came flooding over me. But it was much easier to take in the daytime. And knowing I'd survived the most horrible night of my life helped me to stay calm and circle through all my options again. Of course, I ended up just where I'd started.

Finding these things is *your only way out.*

So I sat up and ate a can of Vienna sausages while I formulated a plan.

• • •

I assumed the land would continue getting higher south and southeast of me. Somewhere in that direction was also my way out of the hammock and back to civilization. I would start exploring that way and try to find signs of Bigfoot.

I left my poncho and backpack and set out above the spring with only my knife and another package of peanut butter crackers. The giant cypress loomed far overhead, their branches filtering the sunlight into slivers falling across the palmetto and ferns. I pressed through the underbrush for close to a hundred yards, scanning my surroundings for any sign of the ground sloping up. But everything seemed flat in all directions.

• • •

On that first day I didn't venture far from the spring. And I didn't find any signs of Bigfoot. I don't think I really expected to. Something told me that even though Stanley was crazy, some of the things he said were true. Most of all that I was going to have to put in my time before I had any chance of seeing these creatures.

For supper that evening I sat under the shelter and ate the last of my peanut butter crackers. I had one can of Vienna sausages left before I was completely out of food. I got up and walked over to the spring and knelt beside it and drank the cool water. Then I stared down at the gar. I think I had been counting on them all along. With a little ingenuity I was sure I could figure out a way to get to them. They looked so easy. Like grabbing fish out of an aquarium. The fact I'd have to eat them raw didn't worry me. I'd had sushi before, and I didn't expect they would be much different.

I sat up for a while thinking of ways to catch the gar and studying the night sounds. I was still uneasy in the dark, but I wasn't completely helpless like I'd been before.

Everything I heard, Dad had described to me on at least one of our hunts together. The squalling of a raccoon. The echoing call of a barred owl. The cheeping of tree frogs and the electric buzzing of cicadas. There was nothing I didn't recognize. And nothing I suspected was Bigfoot.

20

THE NEXT MORNING I ATE THE LAST OF THE VIENNA SAUSAGES
for breakfast. Then I walked to the spring and studied the
gar. I tried to count them and got to thirty-three before their
movement caused me to lose track.

*At least thirty-three. A fish per day gets me at least thirty-
three days.*

After a little searching I found a cypress limb that was
long and straight and about the thickness of a broomstick.
My Swiss Army knife had a short saw blade that I used to
cut the limb. Then I whittled one end to a point and
waded into the spring. The fish were quicker than I
expected and easily dodged my jabs. It took me nearly an
hour to finally stab one. I felt it jiggling at the end of the
spear for a second before it slipped off again.

I need a barb.

Fortunately the fish was mortally wounded. As it grew weaker the spring boil drove it toward the surface until I was able to grab it and pull it out. I flipped it onto the ground behind me, careful to avoid its dangerous-looking teeth. Then I turned and sat there staring at it, swelling with confidence. I guessed it weighed close to five pounds. That was plenty of food for a day or more.

I didn't need the fish right away, so I got a thin stick, sharpened one end of it, and punched it through the gills. Then I submerged the gar in the creek and stabbed it to the mud. I reasoned the other gars couldn't get to it, and the spring water would keep it cooler than a refrigerator. The only thing I worried about was a raccoon or some other scavenger finding it, but I hoped the fact it was underwater would keep it hidden.

Clean water and fish. Thirty-three days.

Now I had food and didn't have to worry about digging and eating worms. I set out to do my research that day with new optimism.

• • •

I walked farther into the hammock that morning but found no broken trees or shelters indicating anything like a Bigfoot. Everywhere I went the swamp looked the same, more mud and endless tangles of green. On my way back for lunch, I felt foolish for even looking.

These things aren't something you go out and find. They'll find you when they're ready. When you've earned it.

I retrieved the gar out of the creek and sat with it on the ledge. I made a slit down its belly, pulled out the intestines, and tossed them into the creek where they would wash away. I had helped Dad gut fish a few times before, but he had always cut the fillets. Remembering what I'd seen him do, I cut behind the gills and sliced along the backbone. My knife blade wasn't long enough to do a very good job, but I managed to remove a fillet without wasting too much. I did this to both sides, tossed the leftover carcass, and washed the meat in the spring.

I cut a small sliver of the gar and set it on my tongue. It certainly tasted like raw fish. I reminded myself of the tuna sushi I'd eaten and began to chew, imagining the taste was no different. The meat was soft and a little sticky and smelled and tasted much stronger than tuna. But it wasn't too bad. I swallowed and put another slice into my mouth.

• • •

I ate the entire raw gar for lunch. The taste of it stayed in my mouth, and for the first time in days I missed having a toothbrush. But I felt the energy of it immediately, and something about the clean, pure, uncooked meat I'd obtained with a spear made me feel that much closer to my goal.

In some of the BSO reports I'd read, people mentioned the creatures hitting trees with large sticks to communicate. After lunch I went in search of a suitable branch to whittle into a club. Not far from the spring, I found a cypress limb that had been broken off by another falling tree. It was still fresh and green and just the right size for what I wanted. I sawed away a four-foot section and took it back to the ledge. I spent the rest of the afternoon stripping the bark and tapering one end down until it was shaped like a baseball bat.

On one of our walks, Dad had told me about eating the root of palmetto. He said it tasted like artichoke. So just before dark I dug up one of the plants with my knife and cut off the root. I shaved away the outer layer to reveal the palm heart. It was only as long and thick as my little finger, but it tasted good and I was encouraged to have at least one other thing to eat besides raw gar.

I spent the last minutes of daylight resharpening my knife blade on the limestone ledge. Then I took the bat and withdrew into the shelter. I sat against the tree with it in my lap and stared over the spring as darkness fell. The hammock was soon alive with its usual night sounds, which didn't intimidate me nearly as much. I gripped the bat, optimistic about using it to call the creatures but also feeling a newfound sense of security.

• • •

I sat there without moving, staring out from under the shelter into the grainy darkness, waiting for the moon to come up. I reasoned Bigfoot was more active at night, like most other predators. About nine o'clock I saw the top edge of a quarter moon peeking above the hammock canopy. Then, slowly, it rose into the night sky, casting the refuge in a faint bluish light.

At ten o'clock I crawled out of the shelter with the bat. I walked around the back side of the oak tree and stood there for a moment, listening and contemplating what I was about to do. Then I raised the bat and hit it lightly against the trunk. The night sounds lowered for a moment as the creatures around me ducked away at the strange noise. I listened but heard nothing unusual. I hit the tree again, harder this time, the loud crack traveling across miles of emptiness. And I imagined somewhere out there, they were listening.

21

I STOPPED SEARCHING FOR THE CREATURES AND STAYED AT the shelter. I ate raw fish and palmetto and lay around under blue skies and rain, watching the spring and the trees and the fall breezes rustling the canopy. I had dreamy thoughts of my parents. Sometimes I thought I heard their voices in the breeze, and it reminded me of places and times I'd been with them. And afterward I cried quietly to myself, poisoned with loneliness.

Every night I made four or five wood knocks after the hammock had slipped into deep darkness. In the daytime there was little sound, except for the gurgling spring. I felt the rest of the world drift away from me, like it was something I would never be part of again. Sometimes I spoke out loud just to hear my voice. I wasn't hungry, but I felt myself slowly starving, like it didn't matter if I ate or not. Like no matter how long the food lasted, I had come there to die, and meanwhile there was nothing to live for except to make the wood knocks and hope these things showed themselves. And even then, I was no longer sure what I would do if that happened. I seemed to have forgotten what finding these things was going to fix.

As the days continued to pass, I grew physically weaker, but my senses grew stronger. The different bird calls and insect noises and animal feeding habits became so predictable that I didn't even need my watch to tell me what time of day it was. I could forecast the weather by detecting subtle changes in the temperature and moisture and breezes. I could taste the wetness of the air and feel the thickness of it as I breathed it in.

I began to smell the smallest of things I'd never thought carried an odor. One day I was sleeping by the spring and into my nose flowed a scent like dirt with a sprinkling of black pepper. Before I even opened my eyes, I knew I was about to see a bullfrog inches from my face.

Even the plants had their own unique scent. The palmetto had more of a sour smell and the fern more bland. The cabbage palm smells of lilies, the cypress a sweet balsamic, the sweetgum like apples, and the oak a heavy, smoky smell. And all of this mixed together to form the general aroma of the air, which varied with the breezes.

Another day I looked at my reflection in the spring and saw what looked like a stranger. His cheeks were hollow-looking, and his eyes were sunken and blank. The skin was blackened with smudged dirt and sap, and his hair was scraggly and stiff. I looked at my hands and saw my fingernails, caked with dirt and grime. My clothes were torn and stained and barely clung to me. I couldn't remember the last time I'd changed. I couldn't remember thinking at all about being clean. The word seemed to have no place here. Like books and radios and paintbrushes. Clean didn't have anything to do with life and death.

I felt the stitches on my face and tugged at the sutures. This time there was no pain. I used my knife and my reflection to cut them and pull them from my skin. When I was done I ran my hand over my face and felt the puckered edges of the scars. I didn't care if they eventually went away or not. It didn't seem to matter.

• • •

I was out there two weeks before something strange happened. It was close to ten o'clock at night. I had made a few wood knocks but, as usual, had heard no reply. I was sitting in front of the shelter, bat in my lap, watching the tops of the cabbage palms swaying gently against a sky of endless stars. Most of the time, in addition to the other night sounds, I heard owls calling in the distance. But despite the usual insect chatter going at full volume, the owls were silent. For some reason I decided to try to call to them to see if I could get a response. I cupped my hands around my mouth, lifted my chin, and gave my best imitation of a barred owl.

Whoo whoo-whoo whoo—whoo whoo—whoo whoooo.

Within seconds I heard what sounded like an owl call back to me. The response was distant and faint but unmistakable. Then I called again. A moment later I got another response, but this time it was much closer. Close enough that I could really hear it. Then an eerie feeling slipped over me, a feeling that something wasn't quite right about the sound. I'd heard the owls for so many nights that their calls were burned into my memory. This call was too loud and deep and guttural. Almost as if it were not an owl at all, but a large man trying to imitate one.

I quickly slipped back into the shelter and sat there, facing my doorway, clutching the bat. I realized that now even the insects had gone silent. There was no sound except for the spring. There had been the initial shock of my realization, but now a slow upwelling of fear crept through my body. The fear of a heavy, unseen presence stalking me. And I sat quietly trembling for what must have been an hour, hearing and seeing nothing. Until the insect chatter finally rose again, and I sensed I was alone once more.

• • •

Although the owl-calling incident was terrifying, I suspected I'd finally made first contact. But it took me all of the next day to commit to trying it again. I had to keep reminding myself that despite my fear, no harm had come to me. Above all else, making contact with the creatures was what I had come to do. If I couldn't face them, I might as well quit it all and return home no better off than when I'd left. And I wasn't ready for that.

For two more nights I made the owl calls. I got no response, but I sensed they were out there. I think now they had been there all along, watching me grow weaker by the day. I began to know when they were nearby. Imagine you are alone in a dark forest with a radio playing the night sounds of crickets and frogs and tiny birds cheeping in the brush. Then imagine someone slowly turning the radio down until there is no sound at all except the soft bubbling of a spring beside you. That's when I knew they were close. But I also *felt* their closeness. The fear of them rose in me as if long ago these things had hunted men and their presence still aroused some primeval alarm.

The next time they responded to my calls, I knew there was more than one of them. I heard three distinct owl imitations from different directions. The closest one couldn't have been more than a hundred yards away. As usual the night had gone silent, and fear began to smother me. Yet this time, when I crawled into the shelter, I thought I heard something grunt behind me. I listened and breathed deeply, trying to get past my fear and take in the scent of the thing—the acrid stench I'd read about on the BSO website. But I smelled nothing except the heavy green and rot of the hammock.

I decided not to imitate the owl the following night to see what would happen. The creatures still came. And continued to come for another two weeks without me calling at all.

Sometimes I thought I saw dark shadows moving on the opposite side of the spring. I certainly sensed and heard them. I listened to their grunts and the snapping of twigs. Other nights I felt and heard nothing. The swamp sounds played at full volume, like the creatures weren't there at all, gone perhaps miles away to other parts of the Refuge.

During the day I found their footprints circling the perimeter of the spring. They were just like I'd seen on the internet—imprints of humanlike feet, broad and mostly flat with a distinctive crease in the middle. Some of them were as much as twenty inches long.

My fear of the creatures lessened each night and was replaced by anticipation. Despite all the activity, I had yet to see anything more than shadows. I was so optimistic about seeing them that I ignored a more immediate problem facing me: I had run out of fish.

There were still more gar in the spring, but they were too scattered and I was too weak to catch them. Then I broke my knife blade digging for palmetto root. Strangely none of this bothered me. I was gradually approaching my goal, as vague as it had become. Nothing else seemed to matter except hanging on as long as I could until I saw these things. And maybe I couldn't hang on that long, and maybe it didn't matter anyway.

I began to eat frogs. Just after sunset, when I heard them cheeping, I crawled around the edge of the spring with my penlight and blinded them and hit them with my spear. They were slippery and slimy to hold but soft enough that I could grip them by the head and bite through their thighs. The rest of the frog was mostly intestine, so I tossed it away and chewed and swallowed the leg meat and spit out the bone.

I often wondered if I was going crazy. Then I remembered that if I was crazy, I wouldn't know it. I wondered if maybe I wanted to go crazy. Maybe that was part of what I had to do. And then my thoughts went in circles, trying to remember where I had come from and what I was doing out there.

I was only certain of one thing. There was nothing more I could do. And I thought I was prepared for what was about to happen. I thought I'd slipped into such a state of weak resolution that even fear itself had been starved out of me. I was wrong.

22

IT HAD BEEN SEVERAL DAYS SINCE I'D HEARD ANYTHING FROM the creatures. I sat outside the shelter listening to the night sounds playing at full volume, sensing nothing, having no reason to suspect they were nearby. Out of boredom and impatience, I decided to imitate the owl again. As my call echoed over the hammock, I listened. A moment later I got my response, but it wasn't at all what I expected. They were tired of playing games, and they let me know it.

From directly across the spring came a howl that nearly rolled me over. Calling it a howl is the only way I know how to describe it, but it's much more than that. If you've ever been next to a train when it blows its horn, then you might have some idea of what this noise is like. Then imagine it being even louder than that. The sound vibrated my insides, like I was in a car going over a corduroy road. It seemed to go on forever, penetrating every part of me and making me physically ill. I got onto all fours and began puking. What little food I had in me came up and then I was dry heaving at the ground. The next thing I remember is waking up outside the shelter with sunlight on my face, staring up at oak leaves.

The howl changed everything for me. Up until then I was thinking of these creatures as something flesh and blood, something I could understand. Like a bear or a wolf but larger. The sound this thing made was not earthly. I had no basis for it. It went far beyond just a sound. It was as much a weapon as anything else. Somehow the howl was at a frequency designed to overload my senses—to bring physical harm to my body.

If I could have left then, I would have. But it was too late. I didn't have the strength to fight my way through days of tangled swamp and water. My penlight was already fading, and I suspected I had maybe one or two more nights to use it.

• • •

Little did I appreciate the security and comfort that glow of light had given me. Once it was gone, I felt I'd lost all connection with humankind. I spent the nights lying in terror. Terror that played in my head like a distant wailing siren, overlaying and smothering all logical thought and reason. There was no defense against it. There was nothing to do but ball up and clench my teeth and squeeze my eyes shut against the darkness.

I lost track of the days. I stopped eating, and my stomach cramped with the pains of starvation. Occasionally I crawled down to the spring and drank. Then I lay beside the water for hours, watching the gar hanging in the clear depths and insects crawling in the reeds and whatever else happened to be in front of my eyes. Sometimes I fell asleep until I felt rain on my face or the cold night air. Then I crawled back to the shelter, curled up on the palmetto fronds, and pulled my jacket over me.

At some point I noticed the face of my watch was broken and the hands no longer moved. I think I might have hit it against the limestone ledge. I didn't care. I no longer cared about the time, about hours and minutes. There was only day and night. And waiting in between.

One afternoon I took off the watch and flipped it into the spring and saw it sink slowly until it bumped into the wall and slid down into the black abyss. Later on it occurred to me I could have used the watch hands to make a fish hook. Then it seemed like too much work, and I was glad not to have the temptation.

• • •

Finally, after I don't know how many days, I saw one. I woke in the night, immediately aware something wasn't right. I had fallen asleep next to the spring. I heard the water gurgling beside me, but the frogs and the insects and the night birds were absolutely quiet. I lay on my back, staring up, but I saw no stars. Everything over me was inky black. Then I thought maybe I was dreaming. But I breathed deep and inhaled the full scent of the beast.

The smell was an odor of rotten meat and urine so heavy and thick it made me gasp. And when I made that small noise, I detected something about the darkness shift above me. Then I felt the breath of it fall over my face. It was the breath of a dog, but stronger and meatier.

As I slowly focused my eyes, I began to make out white teeth and then the full features of the creature leaning over me, not ten inches from my nose.

Now he's going to eat me.

What I saw bore some resemblance to a man's face, but in the most gruesome way. The teeth were square like human teeth but four times as big. Cartoonishly exaggerated. The mouth was horrendously wide. The jaw, if opened, could fit my head into it. The nose was as large as my fist but pressed in like a fighter's nose that's been broken many times. The eyes were glossy black with no trace of iris or pupil.

I was paralyzed. I couldn't even breathe. I was looking at a monster. The terror I felt was so great I wanted to die to escape it.

23

THE BEAST STARED AT ME FOR WHAT FELT LIKE AN ETERNITY.
Then the face withdrew, and I watched the creature rise
before me to its full height, outlined by the starry night
sky. Even though I'd seen and read about and expected
something this big, I wasn't prepared for the enormity of
it. He was every bit of ten feet tall with shoulders five feet
apart.

I must have started breathing again, because my lungs
filled with the stench of him. Then he made a clicking
sound, and I heard something moving in the underbrush
to my left. He took a small step sideways and crouched
about six feet away, facing me. It seemed strange that
something that big could move at all and make no noise.
And it struck me just how fluid his motions were.

I cocked my eyes and watched him. The beast was hunched over and working on something with his hands. Then I heard a snap and a wet tearing sound. I saw him lift something to his face, and his mouth opened to reveal the giant teeth in the starlight. Then I heard him crunching and smacking. I was still in such a state of numb shock that, for an instant, I wondered if he had pulled off my leg and taken a bite of it. Then I realized he was too far away.

I heard another series of clicking sounds come from the underbrush. Each of the clicks had its own distinct tone, and the noises strung together sounded like a strange language. The beast stopped chewing and looked to his right. He clicked back. I heard more movement and thought I saw the shadow of something large cross above the ledge.

The beast must have stayed there five or ten more minutes, with me listening to him smack and chew and occasionally getting glimpses of his white teeth. Then he suddenly stood and took one step and disappeared into the underbrush with barely a sound. It wasn't natural, the way this thing moved. It was like a bulldozer driving quietly through a thicket. It made no sense.

I waited until the chorus of crickets and frogs rose around me again, and I knew he was gone. Then I sat up and looked past my feet. I saw the mound of something lying on the ledge. I got to my knees and crawled to it cautiously. It took me a moment to determine what I was looking at. A deer with its hind legs torn away, its dead eyes reflecting in the sky glow. The top half of the carcass looked untouched. I reached out and ran my hand along its fur. After a moment I crawled closer and got over the back of it, where blood was puddled on the ledge. I inhaled the coppery smell of raw meat and the scent flowed into my body like warm soup, alerting and reviving every dying organ inside me. With no hesitation I lowered my head and began to eat.

• • •

The beast had left me a gift. It was the last thing I expected. I ate my fill of venison that night and puked and ate again and puked again. It wasn't a sick feeling, but more like my body refused to hold food. Later the doctors would tell me a stomach shrinks when a person is starving, and it takes time to stretch it out again. Even though I couldn't keep anything down, it satisfied me just to taste the meat and feel the sustenance of it permeating my bloodstream.

• • •

My body was still weak when I woke the following morning, but my mind felt healthier than ever. It seemed as if the sun was brighter and the birds louder. The carcass lay just beyond the front of the shelter, the limestone still wet and sticky with blood. I saw it was a doe, something I hadn't noticed the night before.

I had a smaller blade on my knife no bigger than half my little finger. I used it to cut into the deer's shoulder and slice off more of the venison. This time I was able to keep it down by swallowing small portions and waiting ten to fifteen minutes between bites.

I guessed the temperature was in the midsixties, cool and comfortable for me but probably not cool enough to keep the meat from spoiling within a couple of days. I sat there until nightfall, eating when I could, trying to regain my strength. And while I waited for the food to settle, I thought about the beast and tried to get my head around what I'd seen and why he had acted the way he had. He was flesh and blood. He ate and he breathed. But there was something more to him. The size of him. How agile and quiet he was. Had I not heard them occasionally crack a twig or crunch in the leaves, I would have considered them ghostlike. And then there was the howl. I felt like it could have stopped my heart with it, had it done that in my face.

For two more days I ate the venison, feeling my body growing steadily stronger. I was careful to cut into a new area of the carcass each morning to avoid those parts that had become covered with flies. I got no sense that the creatures were around, but I no longer trusted my instincts when it came to predicting them. And should they decide to show themselves, there was nothing I could do about it.

As my body and mind became stronger, I circled back to my old reasoning about why I had come out here. And for the first time in over a month, I thought about the camera in the backpack. I pulled it out and looked it over. Just holding it in my hands, I felt like I was dangerously pushing my luck. If they had any concept of what a camera was and what I planned to do with it, I was certain they would let me die or kill me. I shoved it back into the backpack and tried to put the idea out of my mind. Then I thought it strange that I would even consider these things knew what a camera was.

In my mind I began referring to the one who brought me the deer as Andre, after a wrestler I'd seen on television called Andre the Giant. I assumed it was a male and suspected this same creature was the one I'd seen that night long ago. But I knew there were others. And I was about to meet them.

24

ON THE THIRD DAY AFTER MEETING ANDRE, I FELT AS IF I WERE
being watched again from the moment I crawled out of
the shelter. The feeling is both mental and physical. There
is an unexplained heightened fear that comes with a grad-
ual suffocation of the senses, a soft ringing in the ears,
shortness of breath, and a quickening heartbeat. But I
didn't expect the creatures to come around in the daytime,
so I told myself I was just imagining things and overly
anxious about their return.

Despite my uneasy feeling, I decided to get on with
another day of trying to survive. I was getting worried
about the venison. There was still a lot of meat left, but
almost the entire carcass was covered with flies. I decided it
was too risky to keep eating off it, but I had another plan.

I cut off a small piece of meat and tossed it into the spring. I watched it sink slowly until one of the gars approached and snapped it up. Convinced they would take it as bait, I dragged what was left of the deer to the edge of the spring and pushed it in. Then I got my spear and positioned myself near the floating carcass and waited.

Suddenly I heard a crashing sound over my shoulder. In an instant Andre was beside me. He reached and swiped the carcass out of the water and hurled it into the trees. It all happened so fast, I barely had time to roll away and lie on my back and stare up at him. My body was weak, my mind was wrecked, and I was totally helpless. But for the first time, I was able to fully take in his features.

In daylight he was even more impressive. He stands slightly slumped, like someone with bad posture, and his arms hang just a little in front of him. I focused on his hands first. They are proportioned like human hands, but as large as baseball mitts, and the tops are covered with coarse black hair like the rest of his body. The fingernails are brownish-yellow and hard and chipped, like he uses them for digging. His arms are longer in proportion than a man's, like gorillas, the hands hanging almost at the level of his knees. The biceps are as big around as my waist. The chest is barrel-shaped without an inch of fat on it, ripped like a bodybuilder but three times the size of Andre the Giant. Over all the muscle is longer hair, nearly three inches long. Beneath it is leathery, ash-colored skin. He appears to have no neck, and while his head is still three times the size of a man's, it seems too small for the body—like a bowling ball lodged between two massive shoulders. But it isn't round—it's more egg-shaped, with a high forehead. There's more hair around the face but not on it. The heavy brow line makes him vaguely resemble a Neanderthal man, yet there's something slightly off about the spacing of his facial features. The eyes are too far apart, and the nose is too high above his mouth. But the nose is hooded like a human's. While I was staring at him, the nostrils flared in and out, like he was constantly taking in my scent. Through the enormous mouth he sucked and exhaled massive amounts of air with a throat that must be the size of a fire hose. I thought I detected a look of anger, but it was hard to tell. The mouth seems only capable of opening and closing. There are no lips, and it doesn't move at the edges to give away a frown or a smile. All expression is in the nose and eyes. Black eyes as reflective as glassy obsidian.

It occurred to me later that the smell of him wasn't as strong and offensive that time, more like a large, wet dog, exactly the odor you would expect from such a thing. The stronger smell may be a form of defense, like skunks have.

Or it might just be something they emit depending on their mood. It's not just the appearance of these creatures that is hard to accept; there are things about them that go against the laws of nature as we know them. It really is like they are from another planet.

For example, they react and move at an unbelievable speed. Something as big as these creatures shouldn't be able to move like that. As strange as this sounds, their movement reminds me of a mouse. The way mice jump and sprint in spurts and twitches. But that's what it's like. Thousand-pound ape-men that can move as quickly as mice. Like they have so much muscle, they can overcome their mass.

I found another thing unsettling. After Andre hurled away the deer carcass, he stood over me and stared at me for several minutes. I thought he was trying to intimidate me, but I was slipping into that same flawed logic that they think like we do. I don't know why he studied me for so long—there's no pattern to how they act. It's like something really smart and insane and unpredictable at the same time. You can never be at ease or lower your guard around them. And then again, even the notion of guarding yourself is ridiculous. The biggest, strongest human in the world would cower before him, helpless.

A noise across the spring caused the beast to look away.

In my periphery I saw another figure appear from the trees. I slowly turned my head and watched it approach the water's edge. This one was smaller, but still close to six feet tall. I could tell right away that it was a female. The hair covering her body was lighter in color, like that of a golden retriever. Her face looked smooth and young and innocent and not nearly as weathered and monstrous. Like maybe she was a teenager that hadn't yet grown into the gruesome features of the adults. From a distance, there was something captivating about her. In my mind I called her Jane.

Andre made a clicking sound at her. She sat at the edge of the spring and pulled her knees up and hugged them like a kid. Then Andre stepped into the pool and waded out into the clear water until it was chest high. There he stopped with his arms hanging beside him and his back to me. I remained absolutely still, my eyes darting back and forth from the female to what I now assumed was her father. It seemed like nearly ten minutes had passed before Andre's arm appeared to twitch. In fact it had moved several feet out in front of him, but so fast it was barely noticeable. He lifted a gar from the water and tossed it to the female. She snatched it from the air as quickly as a snake strike.

What I saw next caused my initial impression of Jane

to vanish. She watched me as she brought the live fish to her face, her eyes void of all emotion, reminding me of an animal wary of you approaching their meal. Then her mouth expanded eight inches to the outside of her cheeks and opened to reveal that shocking set of square, pearl-white, humanlike teeth. As I looked on in horror, she took a large bite out of the gar's back while it flipped and struggled and quivered. As she studied me and chewed, I heard the crunching of bones and watched blood drip from her mouth and fish scales cling to her lips and teeth. She swallowed and bit the fish again, with no aversion to head, intestines, or tail. And in only a moment, she had consumed every part of it.

I slowly looked away to see that Andre had resumed his fishing posture. A few minutes later he flipped another gar up to the female. This process went on for close to a half hour, resulting in six fish. Jane ate two of them and kept four uneaten beside her. Finally, Andre swam across the deep part of the spring with a sort of dog paddle, but without kicking his feet. As awkward as that sounds, it appeared very fluid and natural. The female stood to meet him, holding two of the fish. Andre stepped out of the water, picked up the other two, and they disappeared into the hammock like I had never been there.

I don't know if they really came to catch fish or if he

was demonstrating the technique to me. Obviously I'm not fast enough—no human is fast enough—to catch fish like that. But he didn't leave any for me or give any sign his actions were meant to teach me anything. The only clear message I got out of the encounter was they considered the spring theirs, and I'd crossed the line by polluting it with the deer carcass.

That afternoon I started to think about the camera again. Now that I knew they would show themselves in the daytime and didn't appear to want to hurt me, I might be able to pull off what I'd come to do. To get such good pictures of these things that it would be impossible for anyone to doubt that they exist.

25

THREE DAYS PASSED BEFORE I SAW THEM AGAIN. DURING THAT
time I found the deer carcass where it was lying nearly
fifty feet away in a palmetto thicket. The meat was certainly spoiled, and now it was covered with both flies and
mud. But I was able to cut more pieces off it and use the
bits of rancid venison to lure two gars close enough to jab
with my spear.

On that third day I was lying on the ledge, doing nothing. Daylight was fading, and long shadows lay across the
clearing. Through the steady thrum of insects and lull of
the trickling water, I felt the sensation of being watched
again.

I turned my head and scanned the other side of the
spring. At first I didn't see anything, but I'd studied the

weave of the sticks and branches and leaves at every time of day for so many days, the pattern of it all was burned into my memory. Only a moment passed before I noticed a hairy black lump that was out of place. With further study I made out glistening eyes in the center of the lump. A chill coursed up my spine as I recognized the face of Andre, who was staring back at me. But it was more the *way* he was staring at me that creeped me out. He was on all fours, positioned with his belly to the ground in a sort of spider-crawl. He wasn't gazing chin-out like any human in a similar posture would have to do—his head was cocked up between his shoulders like it was sitting on top of his back. Like his neck is able to tilt at a ninety-degree angle.

I wondered how many times they'd crawled through the swamp to watch me. I'd heard nothing. Not even the forest creatures had given me warning. I think somehow the hammock animals can sense the mood of the beasts, or perhaps the beasts can quiet them with the infrasound. It just doesn't make sense. But that's how it is. Just when you think you've come to know them, they do something that makes you think you really don't know anything.

I must have studied Andre for five minutes before he suddenly stood. And it wasn't like humans stand—getting to one knee, pushing up from the ground, and straightening. Andre simply folded backward and rose to his full height. The motion was so silent and fluid and unnatural, it was unnerving.

It was obvious the beast knew I'd seen him, but he remained still, continuing to watch me from a standing position. I couldn't imagine what he wanted, but now that he wasn't in the strange spider-crawl and his head was back to normal, I felt my breathing slow and the fear subside. And gradually I came to my senses and thought about the camera.

I began to push myself up slowly. Andre blinked his eyes, and I stopped. It was the first time I noticed he had eyelids. When he made no other move, I sat all the way up. Then I kept watching him while scooting backward toward the shelter. Once I was through the entrance, I looked away for a moment to find my pack. I saw it and no more than touched the zipper before I heard a low, resonant growl that shook my insides. It was a milder version of the deathly howl I'd heard before, but I was instantly queasy and sick. I pulled my hand away from the pack and lay on my side, taking deep breaths, trying to concentrate the nausea away. I could still see him, standing in the same place, watching me. I also saw my knife lying in the leaves in front of my face. To test my suspicion, I slowly reached for it. The growl came again, and I balled up against the pain and plugged my fingers into my ears and closed my eyes.

"Okay," I said softly. "Okay."

When I opened my eyes again, he was still there. The pain in my gut had subsided. I pulled my fingers away from my ears, and all was quiet. The hammock was nearly cloaked in darkness, but the insects and birds and other small animals had ducked away and gone silent.

I detected movement to my right and cocked my eyes to see Jane sitting on the ledge with her knees pulled up again. She was watching me from no less than ten feet away. I took more deep breaths, waiting for the nausea to pass. She smiled, but it wasn't a smile. Her mouth stretched across to slightly reveal the teeth. The smile of a monster. I didn't know what she meant by it.

"I'm Adam," I said quietly.

She glanced across the spring at her father. He made a series of clicking sounds, and she looked at me again.

I've already tried to describe how fast these things can move. But what happened next still shocks me. Sometimes I wonder if I really saw it this way, or if it's exaggerated in my mind because of the sickness they'd given me.

I was staring at the female when I detected movement across the spring. In the time it took my eyes to dart from the female to where her father had been, Andre had leapt the twenty feet from one side to the other and landed in front of me. This went beyond fluid, graceful acrobatics. All I can liken it to is a glitch in a video game. Like a skip in time. But I remember, as my eyes were moving, seeing the frames of him in the air. The distance of the jump and the speed with which it happened and the landing itself were equally unbelievable. When he landed it seemed as if there was not even a bend in his knees. It was all as easy as if someone had taken a simple hop. I would even call it weightlessness had I not felt the tremor of the earth beneath me.

At this point I can't imagine what is going on. What they're thinking and what they're about to do. Nothing about them is predictable. The only thing I was certain of was they weren't going to allow me to touch anything of human making.

Then things got even weirder.

• • •

Andre and Jane were in front of the shelter watching me when I heard the leaves rustling to my left. I was still curled into a ball on the palmetto mat. My queasiness was subsiding, but I was too scared to move. Out of the corner of my eye, I saw another one spider-crawl into view and stop a short distance from the entrance to my shelter. He studied me for a moment, then stood in that strange, hinged way. This one was no more than five feet tall and obviously a young male. In the face he was even more human-looking than the female. Had I not known of these creatures, I would have thought it no more than a chubby six-year-old covered in hair. But a six-year-old who probably weighs two hundred pounds.

He stepped toward me curiously. I found myself studying his feet. They were disproportionately large, like he would wear a size ten shoe. It reminded me of a puppy that hasn't grown into his feet. The feet were also malformed, with the ankle almost in the center of the foot and a heel sticking out several inches. I only noticed this because the others' feet weren't like this. On them the ankle is about where it would be on a human.

The young one approached me and dropped down into the spider position again, and suddenly I was staring him in the face. I no longer noticed his body was covered in hair. What I saw was so human-looking I felt if I spoke he would answer me back in perfect English. But what he did next was not human.

He crawled slowly with his arms and legs splayed out, his head swaying and his body making lizard-like movements. His nose constantly sniffed the air as he slithered closer. In that moment I thought of all the stories I'd heard of mother bears protecting their young. How the slightest threat to their cubs provokes them into attacking. And I felt the weight of Andre's stare and was certain if I made the slightest move, he would rip me to pieces.

The youngster approached to within inches of my face. The rancid smell of sour milk fell over me as I looked into his eyes. They were not so black, but a hazel color, and I barely detected a dark pupil in the center. He leaned in and began to sniff my hair. At the same time I felt his hand find my wrist and grip it and squeeze it tightly. He opened his mouth, and I stared into it. I saw his teeth and the bubble gum pink of his gums. Then he stuck out a stubby, ash-colored tongue and licked up the side of my face.

26

THE YOUNG ONE'S TONGUE WAS LIKE WET SANDPAPER. AS I felt it slide up my cheek, I made a sudden, involuntary gasp. He growled and leapt backward as fast and as fluid as a tree frog. He stood behind his father, hugging one of the enormous legs and peering around it at me. Andre didn't move or make any expression. The female made a clicking sound and rocked from side to side, chimp-like. Then, after a few seconds, Andre turned to leave. The young male trailed behind him, and the female stood and followed. After a moment they had melted into the trees.

The spider-crawling is hard to grasp—how can something that large be so agile on fingertips and toes? But there is even something strange about the way they walk upright.

They swing their arms and bend their knees like humans, but there is more bend to the knees and more of a sliding motion with the feet. It's like someone on snow skis. It's hard to imagine and even harder to imitate.

I started to think of them as intelligent. But it's hard to say if they are more or less intelligent than humans. It's a different kind of knowledge they work with. Somehow, they sense whenever I reach for anything made by humans—it's threatening. Like they can read my thoughts. What they know about the specifics of these items, I can't say. I doubt they know a camera is any less dangerous than a pistol. They are probably as ignorant of these things as I am about their superhuman abilities. Regardless of what they knew or how they knew it, I was left with a disturbing problem; they weren't going to let me take their picture. And without the pictures, there was no reason for me to carry on.

I knew soon that I was going to face the slow descent into starvation again unless the creatures helped me. But I couldn't just stay there and expect them to bring me food. Sometimes they were gone for days. And I remembered what Stanley said about them being migratory. Eventually they might even leave the Refuge.

I had to get the pictures as soon as possible, then I could try to find my way out of the hammock. I had to somehow lie in wait with the camera disguised and ready. I had to do this while I still had the strength to make the journey.

• • •

I figured they would be back within a couple of days. By then I was used to spending hours doing nothing but lying around the shelter, conserving energy. It seemed reasonable to think I could lie in wait with the camera until they returned.

The following day I cut more palmetto fronds and stood them up around the four sides of the shelter, leaving only a small crawl space for the door. Then I gathered several armloads of Spanish moss and draped it from the roof so it hung down and covered any remaining gaps. After a couple hours' work, I crawled inside and saw no sunlight through the walls.

I arranged the camera on a log just inside the shelter and to the right. Then I cut a small hole in the wall to take the picture through. My idea was to lie on the palmetto floor, watching over the spring. As soon as I saw one of the creatures, I would only have to move slightly to my right in order to start photographing them.

I realized my plan wasn't perfect. Because of the way the camera was situated, I was only going to be able to get pictures of them standing across the spring. Anywhere else and they'd be out of sight or close enough to suspect something. It was also going to have to be daylight. I could only imagine what they'd do to me if they saw a flash go off.

• • •

Three days passed. In the early morning hours of the fourth night, I heard the padding of footsteps on the limestone ledge. Then I saw one of them walk past the entrance of my shelter. The hair seemed of a lighter color, and I suspected it was the female, but it was too dark to make out any features. And the walls now covered my range of vision and only allowed me to catch glimpses. I know the creature stopped and sat down not very far from me. Even though I couldn't see it, I heard it picking at and eating something. Occasionally it grunted softly. There may have been others, but I was only certain of this one.

For nearly an hour I lay in the shelter, listening to the creature. Everything was peaceful. The night sounds thrummed steadily, and there seemed to be none of the normal signs of danger. But it made me uneasy not to be able to see it, and I was too frightened to move.

Suddenly the night was shattered into silence by one of the fearsome howls echoing across the hammock. I felt the hair on the back of my neck stand up. It seemed far away, maybe a mile or more, but it was enough to send even the beast outside my shelter crashing off through the palmettos.

The howl came again, closer now, perhaps only a half mile away. If it was the same creature, then it had traveled an incredible distance in an impossible amount of time. That paralyzing feeling of helplessness and impending doom gripped me.

I heard and felt it coming at the same time. If you have ever been close to a horse running, then you know how you can feel their footfalls shaking the ground. It felt like that but more powerful. And the sound was like someone driving a truck at high speed through the underbrush. Then the noise and violence increased until I heard what sounded like a tornado all around me, trees snapping and leaves flying. Whatever it was panted and grunted and thrashed about, tearing at the swamp in a complete rage for what felt like five minutes or more. Then the shelter exploded around me, leaves and sticks and palmetto flying around my face. I was suddenly exposed, lying under open sky while the beast raged around me, tearing trees from the ground and hurling them in all directions. This was not Andre. This creature was much bigger. And there was nothing I could do but ball up and wait to die.

27

THE CREATURES HAD MADE ME FEAR FOR MY LIFE SEVERAL
times, but in that moment I thought I was certainly going
to be torn to pieces. I could see no other outcome after this
beast had traveled at least a mile in fury to confront me.

I don't know how long I waited for it to be over. It
could have been only a minute, or it could have been ten.
But eventually he stopped his tantrum, and I heard him
standing over me, taking rough, raspy breaths so deep and
tonal I felt them in my bones. This time I smelled the hor-
rid odor, and I opened my eyes and took in what was no
less than twelve feet of terror, muscled and sculpted like
the largest bodybuilder you can imagine. What looked
like white scars ran across his chest and down his legs, like
he'd spent a lifetime battling other creatures. For the first

time in my life, I felt I was staring into the face of absolute evil. I had never even used that word in my head. I had never understood it until that moment. But now I was facing an entity who craved bringing the fear of death more than death itself.

He leaned over me and opened his mouth. His teeth were white and wet and glistened in the sky glow. He bowed his arms out, clenched his fists, and inhaled. His arms tensed, and every muscle in his body seemed to inflate as he sucked an impossibly long breath into the barrel of his chest. I knew what was coming, and I looked away and slammed my hands over my ears. But there was no defense against it. The scream was so loud and impactful, it caused my body to physically overload and pass out.

• • •

The next thing I knew, I had sunlight on my face. I felt sick and weak and disoriented. I watched the trees overhead for a while, not wanting to move. Eventually I sat up and looked around, queasiness pooled in my stomach. Complete destruction lay before me for twenty feet in all directions. Palmetto and vines and branches were strewn everywhere. Trees a foot in diameter were floating in the spring. There were more jammed up into the branches of other trees.

I started crawling around in a daze, digging in the debris for my pack and camera. The first thing I saw was my bat, broken into three pieces, like he'd found it and focused on it. A moment later I recovered the pack under a fallen tree. Then I had to stop and vomit and lie down to rest. It took me another hour to find the camera. And by the time I did, I wondered why I had even bothered to search for it. But I was too frazzled to make sense of what I was doing. I stuffed it into the pack. And just that small effort had me puking again. I lay on my side, clutching my stomach and waiting for whatever it was to pass.

• • •

I slept for a few hours. When I woke I was still weak, but the sickness had passed enough for me to think straight. I got up and went down to the spring and drank. The cool water helped revive me. Then I sat at the water's edge and tried to figure out what had happened.

I had met the alpha. Of that much I was certain. But why this creature had suddenly acted that way toward me was a mystery. Maybe the female was really his offspring, and he felt threatened by her interest in me. Or maybe he had just found out about me from the others and wanted to show me who was in charge. I didn't know. These creatures just seemed to go ballistic for no reason. And I knew

I couldn't bear another encounter with him. It was worse than death. It was time to leave no matter where I had to go to escape. No matter what was waiting for me back in civilization.

This is over.

I began to plan how I was going to get out of there. I reached into my pocket to grab my knife with the compass, but it wasn't there. An alarming feeling shot through me. I shoved my hand into my other pocket. Nothing. Then I remembered I had it sitting beside my pack in the shelter.

I went back to where the shelter had been and got on my hands and knees. I crawled around, desperately looking for the knife. I reasoned that surely something so small and weighted like that wouldn't be far. But even after clearing the leaves and debris to bare dirt, I didn't see it.

With no compass I knew there was little chance I'd make it out of the hammock alive. I needed to know exactly which way was southeast, the most direct route to civilization. I couldn't afford to make a rough guess using the sun and the stars. I had to make it fast before I ran out of strength. I was certainly too weak to risk getting lost.

I stood up and tried to calm myself, to come up with a logical search plan for the knife. I gazed around the clearing again, taking in the circumference of destruction

Alpha had left behind. This time I noticed something I had missed while crawling around that morning. There was a blue shirt caught up in some branches at the edge of the clearing, gently swaying in the breeze. I didn't remember having any clothes out. Unless they were drying, I always stored them in my pack. And then I realized I didn't have a blue shirt at all.

I slowly approached. As I got closer the shirt became vaguely familiar to me. A blue short-sleeve button-down with a light plaid pattern. It was Dad's.

28

I TOOK THE SHIRT OFF THE BRANCH. MY HANDS WERE trembling as I looked at the tag inside the collar. I already knew what I was going to find. Mom always wrote our names there. It was barely recognizable because of the faded ink, but there it was—*Parks*.

I looked up quickly and slowly turned and searched in all directions. "Dad!" I said aloud.

There was nothing but the endless hammock.

I had not really believed my parents might be alive. Not even once. But now I had Dad's shirt. *Did the creatures find it? How would it have come off him? How would they have found it without finding Dad? And what about Mom? Are they out here? What would Dad be doing without his shirt?*

It didn't make sense. *But the creature left it for me. That's what she was doing last night. There was no way I could leave. If my parents were out there, I had to find them. And to do that, I had to find the creatures.*

It was a quick, easy decision. There was really nothing else to consider. I was going to find my parents or die trying. I stuffed the shirt into my pack and pulled out my cap and slipped it on. Then I gazed over the spring at the spot where the creatures seemed to appear most. That was the best place I knew of to start. Even without the compass I knew I'd be walking roughly north, deeper into the Refuge and almost in the opposite direction of any civilization. But once again, there was no other option.

I circled the spring and arrived at a small gap in the underbrush. I pushed through to find an obvious footpath leading away from the clearing. I was certain it hadn't been there the first day I'd gone looking for shelter and other signs. Yet now here it was, a muddy trail of footprints worn like a cow path.

I stepped into the shadows of the hammock and began following the trail. At first it was obvious. In addition to the giant footprints and matted palm fronds, on either side were twisted and broken branches. But after about a hundred yards, the path diverged in several directions. I stopped for a moment, trying to decide what to do. I looked up at the sky to discern what direction I was headed in. I knew I'd started off going north, but after winding around on the trail I was disoriented. Now I found the canopy so thick all I saw were bits of sunbeam falling across the upper leaves. Without being able to see the sun and without a compass, there was no way to set a course.

I considered retracing my steps. I stood there looking around and listening and thinking. A soft breeze filtered its way through the palms. My eyes were drawn to an area of thick underbrush that wasn't moving. I studied this place and gradually made out the shape of the young female, standing as still as a statue, her golden coat blending in perfectly with tree bark and palm fronds and sunlight. At first the sight of her was shocking. Then it was eerie.

We stared at each other for what must have been a full minute before I heard her grunt softly. I thought of the shirt in my pack. I slowly slipped my arms out of the straps, keeping my eyes on her the entire time. I placed the pack in front of me and knelt behind it and stopped. She made no move. I slowly brought my hand to the zipper and began to open the pack. When she didn't react, I reached inside and felt the shirt on top and eased it out. Then I stood and held it up where she could see it.

The female turned and stepped away and was gone.

"Wait!" I called out.

I hurried after her, stuffing the shirt into my pack again. I came to the place where she'd been standing and stopped and looked around. It took a moment, but I eventually saw her, watching me from about the same distance. I eased the pack on again and waited to see what she would do.

"Do you understand me?" I said.

She didn't respond.

"You brought me the shirt. My dad's shirt. Do you know where my parents are?"

She turned and walked away.

I knew she didn't understand what I was saying, but I was certain she knew what I wanted. And she knew I would follow her to get answers.

• • •

She never let me get closer than forty or fifty feet before she disappeared again. I could tell we were traveling in mostly a straight line, but she led us through dense thickets of cane that I had to fight through and bogs where I sank up to my knees in mud. For what felt like a quarter of a mile, she led me through a shallow marsh, where I waded through black water reaching my waist. It was only when we were in the water that I could see any sign of her moving ahead of me. And then all I saw were the ripples of her passage gently lapping against the flooded timber. She was there and she was gone. Then she was there again and gone again. I would have never traveled through such a place alone. I was certain there were alligators and snakes watching me from every direction.

After what felt like hours of this, I was at the point of exhaustion and about to drop in my tracks. But weak as I was, I had to keep going. I knew if I lost her not only would I never learn the mystery of Dad's shirt, but I would be hopelessly stranded. So I pressed on, sometimes falling on my face in the water, other times tangled in briars or tripping through mud as thick and sticky as tar.

She always waited for me. We eventually came to an area of higher ground, where my feet weren't getting stuck in the mud and the walking was relatively easy. But I was so tired I could barely take a step. Then I tripped over a fallen limb and lay on my side. I didn't think I was going to be able to get up again. I rolled over and saw her stopped ahead, watching me.

"I have to rest," I muttered.

Nothing about her facial expression ever changed. I can't recall even seeing her eyes blink.

I lay there, catching my breath, my legs aching and my stomach sick. After a few minutes I pushed myself up and backed against a cabbage palm. I looked up at the sky. I still couldn't fully see the sun, but I could tell it was after noon. Then the creature grunted softly, and I looked over at her. It struck me again just how human she looked from a distance. She seemed to be about my age.

I made a clicking sound with my mouth, trying to imitate their language. The female didn't react, and I wondered what I'd said, if I'd said anything at all. A moment later she grunted and turned and disappeared. The thought of finding my parents came rushing over me again, and I stood weakly.

"I'm coming," I said.

29

I FOLLOWED FOR WHAT MUST HAVE BEEN ANOTHER MILE OVER
this higher ground. We traveled mostly what looked like
deer trails weaving along under live oaks and loblolly pines
and through palmetto and wispy thickets of cane. Then
we came to a place where I saw a crudely made lean-to
structure off to my right. I stopped and studied it. Several
broken limbs were supported across the upturned root system of a fallen sweetgum. There was a back wall made of
sticks and palmetto. In the hollow space was a mat of
grass, pressed like something as large as these creatures had
recently rested there. I looked for the female and saw another
similar structure on my left. Neither of the shelters were
complete enough to provide much protection from the rain.
They struck me more as temporary outposts.

I heard the beast grunt. I searched the sun-dappled

tangle of underbrush ahead until I saw her dark eyes studying me. I started forward again.

We were getting close to something.

• • •

I felt like I was walking on harder ground. Then I began to see patches of exposed limestone through the leaves. A moment later I broke into a clearing about fifty feet wide, shaded beneath the fronds of giant cabbage palms. Here the limestone rose into a small hill with several flat, boulder-size rocks strewn about. Across the clearing the female sat on her heels, arms wrapped around her knees, like we were stopping. I took off my pack and dropped it on the ground and sat down to rest.

"What is this place?" I said to her.

She didn't blink. Nothing about her moved.

"What about my parents?"

A light breeze passed over me, and I watched her hair flutter around her face. Then the breeze was gone, and her hair fell back into place. After I caught my breath I began looking around the clearing, studying it closely. And I began to pick out subtle things that didn't fit in.

First of all, it seemed odd that the limestone rocks appeared to have been swept clean while the edges of the clearing were thick with oak leaves. I thought maybe the wind had done this, but the small clearing was mostly sheltered and the rocks were flat enough to hold at least a few of them. Across the clearing to my left, I noticed what looked like a deer skull wedged in the fork of two tree limbs. Then my eyes traveled down the tree to something else. At the base was what appeared to be white cloth.

I looked at the female. Had it not been for the shifting of her hair, she could have been made of stone. I stood and started across the exposed rock, walking toward the tree but angling closer to the creature than I'd been all day. Her head slowly turned and followed me. When I came within several yards of the white cloth, the realization of what I was looking at hit me suddenly and caused me to gasp and stop short. There, folded and stacked at the base of this tree, were the rest of my parents' clothes. Mom's white blouse. Her blue jeans. Dad's khaki pants. Everything but their shoes.

I looked at the creature again.

"Where are they?" I said.

Her face gave no answer. I went to the clothes and knelt before them and lifted each folded garment just to make certain I wasn't imagining things. They were stained and torn, but there was no doubt about them being my parents'. Then I began to get a strange feeling about the clearing and didn't like having my back to it. I pulled my hands away from the clothes and looked up past her and over to the giant rocks on the ground behind me and to my right. Not far from the rocks, I saw the beginning of a fissure. The crack gradually widened to about a foot before the boulders covered it. I looked at the female again, like she might have an explanation. But I got nothing from her.

I stood again and walked toward the crack. I was no more than ten feet from my strange guide when I stopped and peered into the outside edge of a dark chasm. When I breathed I sucked in a whiff of death.

My heart began drumming in my chest so hard I could feel it in my ears. I knelt at the edge of the chasm and lowered my face, trying to peer under the boulder and see into the black recesses, but I couldn't see anything. I looked up at the creature again.

"Are they down there?" I asked her.

A breeze tossed her hair around her face again. It was like talking to the trees.

I grabbed the boulder and tried to lift it, but it must have weighed more than a thousand pounds. Not even the strongest man alive could budge it. I lowered my face into the crevasse and breathed in the foul air.

"Dad," I called into it. I got only a deep, hollow echo in return.

30

I ALREADY KNEW THERE WAS NOTHING ALIVE AT THE BOTTOM
of the crevasse. And I knew the remains of Mom and Dad
were down there. I had a passing wish I could see their
bodies, but I knew it was better that I couldn't. I didn't
want to remember them like how they would have looked.

Is this where the creatures hid their own dead?

It was the perfect setup: a deep fissure in stone covered
with a boulder that nothing but a Bigfoot could move. It
would explain a lot about why their remains were never
found. But the fact that they pulled my parents' bodies
from the river, brought them here, and buried them with
their own didn't make sense. And the clothes. *Why fold
them? Who folded them?*

There seemed to be no explanation other than they
have some reverence for life.

I looked at the female again.

"I'm going to get my pack," I said.

I retrieved the pack and returned to the boulder, circling it this time and sitting on the other side of it, facing her. She wasn't more than five feet from me. I put the pack in front of me and slowly opened it and pulled out the blue shirt. When she didn't startle, I held it out to her. She reached and took it. Then she folded it and placed it on the ground between us. The act was both shocking and frightening. I couldn't grasp how she knew to do this unless she'd watched me fold my own clothes. Yet, eerie as it was, it also signaled to me that she was perhaps more curious and accepting of items made by humans than the rest of the creatures.

We watched each other for several more minutes, and all the while, the urge to try something I never thought I would be brave enough to attempt again built up inside me.

I took a deep breath and slowly pulled the camera from the pack. I held it there in front of me for a moment, letting her get a good look at it. It was impossible to tell what she was thinking, but she made no indication I was upsetting her. I slowly raised the camera to my eye and peered at her through the viewfinder. She was right there, only feet away, every detail of her face and body as clear as a photo from *National Geographic*. And I clicked the shutter and she was still there. And I clicked it again. And again. And again. I stood and walked around the boulder and took more pictures of her profile while she sat there, still as a statue. I used every photo and returned to sit down in front of her. I dropped the camera into my pack, breathing heavily, like I'd just let go of a snake. Then I zipped the pack and sat there, trying to calm myself, still in disbelief of what I'd done.

These pictures will be the best photos of a Bigfoot the world has ever seen.

• • •

I wasn't sure what my next move was. Logically I should have been ready to leave. I had everything I'd come for. But there was this creature sitting before me. For some reason she was trying to help me, and I'd betrayed her in a way I couldn't imagine she understood. I couldn't bring myself to just stand and walk away from her after what I'd done. And even if I had, I knew I was hopelessly lost, and without her help I was likely to die before I ever reached civilization again.

The hammock was slipping into the shadows of dusk. I guessed there was only an hour left before nightfall.

"I'm hungry," I said to her.

This close I saw the black of her eyes shimmer in

response to my words, like she took them in but didn't do anything with them.

I brought my finger up and touched my mouth. Suddenly she stood and turned and disappeared into the trees. I assumed she understood what I wanted and was going to find food. I leaned back against the boulder and waited.

She was gone for nearly a half hour before she returned with green trout and placed them before me. She may have already eaten because she didn't seem to want any. She sat down in the same spot and waited.

I wondered if these fish were the rare Suwannee bass Stanley had talked about. Even if they were, it certainly wasn't going to stop me from eating them. Since I didn't have my knife, I had to do as the creatures did and bite into the fish, scales and all. Unlike them, though, I avoided the bones and intestines. There was enough meat on both fish to fill my shrunken stomach without having to chew on the unpleasant portions.

When I finished I wiped the scales from my lips and began to think about where I was going to sleep that night. Then the creature did something strange. She picked up Dad's blue shirt that was still folded next to her and walked it over to the stack of clothes and placed it on top. Then she came back to me and sat again. I'm not sure what she meant by it, but I started to think about the clothes and how they didn't really belong out here and how I should do something with them.

It was almost night now. The crickets were thrumming, and the small animals had ceased scurrying about.

"I'm going to get the clothes," I said.

I stood and went over and picked them up. Then I looked at her to make sure she didn't object for any reason. It was getting hard to see her face in the dark, but she made no movement or sound.

I walked the clothes to the edge of the crevasse and dropped them down the dark hole. I stood there for a moment, thinking maybe I should say a prayer but not sure what was appropriate. Then I remembered Mom had always liked Psalm 23. I didn't remember all of it, but I said what I could recall.

> *The Lord is my shepherd, I shall not want.*
> *He makes me lie down in green pastures.*
> *He leads me beside quiet waters.*
> *He refreshes my soul.*
> *He guides me along the right paths.*
> *Even though I walk through the darkest*
>   *valley, I will fear no evil,*
>   *for you are with me.*

This whole time I had my back to the female. I hadn't heard her move. But when I turned she was standing not two feet from me, looking down at my face. I froze, not knowing what was about to happen. She brought her hand up and placed it on top of my head. Then she slid her hand down the side of my face and onto my chest and stopped there, like she was feeling my heart.

31

AFTER A FEW SECONDS THE CREATURE PULLED HER HAND away and returned to sit at her place near the edge of the trees. I sat down in front of one of the boulders and leaned back against it, facing her and thinking about what had just happened. I believe she was telling me in her own way she was sorry for my loss. I think she also just wanted to touch me out of curiosity. I think she'd been building up the courage for it ever since we'd first met. Then I imagined she was lonely, but I knew I was just trying to give human emotions to something that wasn't human.

How could anyone feel lonely when they'd always been alone?

These creatures live their entire lives with more challenges than loneliness and sorrow and worrying about what people think of them. I believe they simply live to eat and breed and help each other survive for another generation.

Why does it have to be so complicated for humans?

Maybe it doesn't have to be.

"I need you to show me how to get out of here," I said. I pointed over the trees. "Home."

She made a single click that meant nothing to me.

"I can't live out here."

She didn't respond. It was like I was stranded on another planet with an alien who didn't speak my language. Once again I thought back to what Stanley said. *It's like* we're *the aliens, and they've always been here.* And it was true. I was the only alien here.

"Tomorrow," I said to her.

I shoved the cap into my pack, got my jacket out, and lay down and pulled it over me. Then I closed my eyes and drifted off to sleep.

● ● ●

Something woke me in the night. I opened my eyes and saw the creature still sitting against the edge of the palms. She had her head turned, staring off to her left. Then I heard what sounded like the whistle of a bullbat, but something wasn't right about it. I'd been in the hammock long enough to have the sound of every creature burned into my memory, like a record I'd heard over and over thousands of times. The female made the same whistle in response.

I saw a dark form appear between the palms and stop at the edge of the clearing. It seemed like this one was a little taller than the female but not as big as Andre and Alpha. Then I heard another walking beyond the clearing, near where we'd first entered. The first one made a woofing sound I hadn't heard before, and the female stood and returned a series of fast clicks. After that I heard a growl coming from what I thought was about fifty yards into the trees. The female looked at me and grunted. I didn't move. I didn't know what was happening, and it seemed like the creatures were everywhere around me. The growl came again, closer this time. The creature took one step and then she was right in front of me. She bent over and shoved me in the chest. I don't think she meant it to be hard, but I fell backward and rolled onto my side. I lay there for a moment, confused. Then I grabbed the pack, scooted farther away from her, and stood with it. I found myself in the center of the clearing, grunts and growling rising around me. I shouldered the pack and spun in a circle, peering into the dark hammock on all sides. The female approached and shoved me again, and I understood she was telling me to leave. But I didn't know where to go. It sounded like the creatures were everywhere. Suddenly I saw a massive dark body flying through the air like it had come from the trees. It must have been ten feet off the ground. The creature landed between me and the female without a sound. I knew right away it was Andre. And he wasn't happy.

The beast leaned over me and growled, and I felt the sound vibrating in my chest and the queasiness flowing into me. I looked down and stuck my fingers in my ears and began backstepping until I tripped and fell. Then I rolled over and crawled toward the edge of the clearing. Once I was into the trees, I stood and began walking quickly, trying to remain calm. I heard a scream behind me that sounded like the death cries of an old woman. Then the hammock was alive with whoops and grunts and screams, like a pack of angry chimpanzees. I started running blindly, hearing them from all sides, like they were tracking me. I didn't know where I was going—I just knew they didn't want me in that clearing or anywhere close to it.

I didn't think I could be bombarded with any more chaos. But then I heard a howl overlaying everything. I knew right away it was Alpha. And despite the crashing on all sides, I heard him coming through the trees behind me like a tank.

It felt like I had been hit in the back and lifted off the ground with a log. Then I was flying through the air. I saw stars and trees and felt cool wind in my face. There was no pain, and it seemed like time stood still. I'd always heard people talk about your life flashing before your eyes in the moment before death. It happens. In what could have only been seconds, I was with Dad, walking in the woods, listening to him tell me about poison oak. Then I was with Mom, watching her lay out some new clothes she'd bought me. Then we were all together, riding Space Mountain at Disney World. I heard the kids yelling over me and Gantt wrestling on the floor in the hallway. I saw Uncle John sitting alone in his house, worried about me. I saw crazy Stanley on the porch in his wheelchair, staring out into the darkness. And I wasn't angry or upset with any of them. Those issues in that world seemed trivial. That was my world and the only place I could really exist. This was not my world. I would never exist here.

I slammed into the ground and tried to cry out that I wanted to live. That I didn't want to die out here alone. That it was all a mistake, and I should have never come and would never come into their world again. But before I could utter a word, I felt a final blow to the back of my head.

32

I HAD A DREAMY IMPRESSION OF MOVING SWIFTLY THROUGH A swamp at night. There were tree limbs far overhead, and sometimes I caught glimpses of a star-specked sky and a full moon. There was no smell at all. No sound. Only the feeling I was flying, with a cool breeze filtering through my hair.

I woke to full sunlight in my face. I tried to move, and pain shot through my entire body. I tried to call out, but no sound came.

Sometime later I heard voices, and I saw blurred images of people leaning over and staring at me. Then I felt them moving me, and somewhere there was an ambulance and strobing lights, but still no sound.

• • •

Uncle John came into focus, standing over me. I heard the beeping of hospital equipment and the distant murmur of voices.

It was all a dream, I thought. *I never even left this place.*

"Adam," he said.

It was strange to hear my name spoken aloud so close and clear. I tried to respond, but no words came.

Then I dreamt about the hammock, and I heard the frogs and the birds and the bubbling of the spring. I saw the female creature sitting against the edge of the trees, watching me.

"Adam," I heard.

I opened my eyes, and Uncle John was there again.

He put his hand on my shoulder. "Can you talk?"

I tried to speak again. "I don't know," I muttered.

Uncle John smiled at me. "How you feeling?"

I tried to detect any pain in my body but felt nothing. Then I tried to move my head, but it wouldn't work. I blinked.

"I don't know," I said.

"You're pretty banged up."

I tried to make sense of everything, but my thoughts moved sluggishly, like my mind was full of syrup.

"What's wrong with me?"

Uncle John chuckled. "I'm not sure where to start, but you're going to be okay."

"I can't move anything."

"You've got a cast on your right leg and one on your right arm. You've got two broken ribs and three broken fingers."

"Why can't I move my head?"

"The doctor has it stabilized right now, just in case there's a neck injury. He doesn't think there is."

"Am I paralyzed?"

"No, you're fine. It's all just a precaution."

"How did I get here?"

"Some people found you on the roadside outside the Suwannee Refuge. Do you remember what happened?"

I tried, but I wasn't sure about anything.

"I don't know," I said.

"They think maybe you were hit by a car."

"I don't know," I said again.

"Okay, we can talk about it later. I'll go get the doc. He said he'd take the head brace off after you woke up."

• • •

I spent three more days recovering in the hospital. The pain medicine made me sleepy and kept my mind vague and blurry. Uncle John brought me some new clothes and continued to visit before and after work. Dr. Ensley checked on me throughout the day. Sergeant Daniels returned with his notebook. They all wanted to know where I'd been for two months.

I told them I didn't remember anything. But I did. Everything except how I'd gotten out of the Refuge. I suspect the female or Andre carried me, but I'll never know. I told myself I wouldn't talk about it again. That I would live the rest of my life trying to forget, trying to make myself believe it never happened, like Stanley had told me I should do.

Keeping the story of the creatures to myself was easy. Especially since I'd lost all proof of their existence. I knew from experience that mentioning anything about them would only lead to more problems for me. It wasn't so easy when it came to my parents. I knew where their bodies were—at least I had been there. But it would be impossible for me to ever find the place again. And even mentioning that would bring the whole conversation around to Bigfoot.

What was the point in talking about any of it?

Dr. Ensley said I could return to school after a few more days of rest, but it was going to take weeks for my broken bones to heal and all my casts to come off. And I'd probably need a wheelchair for most of that time.

On Thursday Uncle John wheeled me out of the hospital. The late November air was wet and cold and windy, like winter had been holding off, waiting for me to leave the Refuge. But my nose and ears were still too sensitive for city life. The smell of wet asphalt was strong enough to make me gasp. All the smells outside seemed so chemical and intense—rubber and plastics and cooking oils and perfumes. The sounds were metallic and unnatural and made me uneasy.

Uncle John noticed I was acting strange. "You okay?" he asked me.

I nodded.

"You got your teeth clenched."

I opened my mouth and worked my jaw. "I'm fine," I said.

• • •

Uncle John's house looked nicer than I remembered but had a strong antiseptic smell to it. He helped me to my bedroom, and I saw he'd gotten a new bed and desk for me. Against the back wall was a small table with my old television and Xbox.

"Went and got some more of your stuff for you," he said.

"Thanks," I said. Then I looked at the corner of the room, where there was a chest of drawers. Sitting on top was something I never expected to see again.

I pulled away from Uncle John and wheeled myself across the room, stopping in front of the stained and tattered backpack. I stared at it, still not believing it was here. I'd thought about a lot of things since I'd woken up in the hospital, but for some reason, I hadn't thought once about the pack.

"Where did you get this?" I said.

"The people who found you said it was lying on the roadside. They brought it by the house."

I reached out slowly and grabbed the pack and pulled it down into my lap.

"Not much in it," he said.

My heart began to race. "The clothes in there look worse than the ones they found you in. Sure wish you could remember something."

I didn't answer him.

"Maybe there's some pictures on that camera that'll refresh your memory."

33

I TURNED THE CHAIR AND LOOKED AT UNCLE JOHN. I STUDIED
his face, trying to detect any hint that he was joking about
the camera.

"Seriously, Adam," he said. "How can you not know
anything about what happened?"

I didn't answer him.

"Two months. You know what I've been doing for two
months?"

I shook my head.

"I've been driving all over the Florida Panhandle and
clear into Alabama putting out missing person signs. I
nearly lost my job over it. I think I deserve an
explanation."

"I know," I said. "Maybe I'll remember soon."

He stared at me.

"I think I want to be alone," I said.

He nodded and sighed. "All right. Get some rest. I'm headed to work in a couple of hours. Call me if you need anything."

Uncle John left the room and pulled the door closed behind him. I unzipped the pack and reached inside. I felt my cap. My extra shirt. And the camera.

Surely it's broken.

I pulled it out and looked it over. There didn't appear to be anything wrong with it.

• • •

My hands trembled. It was hard to grasp the enormity of what I held. On the camera was possibly the most convincing proof of Bigfoot ever obtained. Close-up photos from every angle of a young female in the wild. It made me nervous just holding it.

I took the camera to my dresser, opened the top drawer, and shoved it under the clothes. Then I shut the drawer and backed away and stared at it. Now I had everything I'd set out to get and more. And I tried to remember what my original plan had been.

Get evidence of these creatures so people don't think I'm crazy. So I don't end up like Stanley.

But it didn't seem so simple now. I thought back to what Stanley had said about the government cover-up.

What if it were true? Could I afford to risk it?

Surely I couldn't simply take the camera to Walgreens and have the pictures developed. What if the government was on the lookout for that kind of thing? My old school had a photo lab, but I no longer attended there, and I didn't even know the photography teacher. On top of all these problems, it was going to be weeks before I could even get around without a wheelchair or crutches.

I didn't know what to do. So I did nothing.

I just got really quiet. I felt the two secrets, the location of my parents' bodies and the Bigfoot photos, swollen and lodged inside me, like tumors I would have to feel and carry the rest of my life.

• • •

On Saturday we had Mom and Dad's memorial service in Perry. Uncle John had been holding off, waiting for me to return. That morning I didn't take the pain pills because I thought they would make me too sleepy during the ceremony.

It was a small gathering, but a few of my old friends from school showed up with their parents. It was strange seeing them. It was strange seeing anybody from my old life. I didn't know what to say and had a hard time making conversation. I looked them in the eyes and heard them speaking, but I couldn't seem to listen to anything they said.

I kept repeating to myself, *You don't even know. You don't know anything.*

They were all so ignorant. Just as I had been. It was impossible for me to see things around me in the same way. Take the Xbox, for instance. If you'd asked me three months before how much I liked playing video games, I would have said it's about my favorite thing to do. Now, that Xbox seemed like the stupidest waste of time I could imagine.

Everything—all the *stuff*—was ridiculous. The televisions we stared at, the cars and trucks we climbed inside of and rode around in. The machines we used to mow our grass and the clothes we put on and the flags we pulled up poles and saluted. *What's it all about? Don't these people know anything? How did everybody get like this?*

After the service Uncle John took me home and helped me to my room.

"How are you doing?" he asked me.

"Everything hurts. Can you get my medicine for me?"

He left and then I heard the water running in the kitchen sink. A moment later he returned with a glass of water and one of my pain pills.

"Thanks," I said.

He watched me while I took it.

"You know you can talk to me about things . . . If you feel like it."

"I'm fine," I said. "There's nothing to talk about."

"I was thinking maybe we could go fishing tomorrow."

Fishing. With a rod and reel. So pointless.

"How am I supposed to go fishing like this?"

"We can—"

"No. I just want to be alone."

He started to say something else but stopped himself. "Adam, would it make you feel better to move back to Perry? I'm just asking. Maybe you'd like to be with your old friends."

I shook my head. "I just want to be alone."

Uncle John nodded like he understood and left my room and closed the door behind him.

The secrets continued to smolder inside me. I sat in the wheelchair and stared out the window. I couldn't stop thinking about the creature who'd helped me and the spring. I still heard the birds and the crickets and the frogs playing in my ears, like I'd never left. Then I fell asleep with my chin on my chest. At some point the pain medicine wore off and the nightmares slipped over me, easy and silent as shadows. I dreamt that I was standing alone in the night beside my old campsite. There was no sound except for the trickling of the spring, no stars and no moon. It was so dark I could barely see the outline of the trees overhead. Then I heard the terrifying sound of Alpha screaming his fit of rage at the night. Coming for me.

I opened my eyes and breathed heavily and stared out the window into the gloam of dusk.

How is this any better? Now I know. I know everything, but nothing is better. I did it all so I wouldn't be like Stanley . . . And now I am Stanley.

34

THE NEXT MORNING I WOKE TO THE SOUND OF UNCLE JOHN
knocking on my door. I opened my eyes and found myself
in bed, staring at the ceiling. My body ached all over, like
I could feel the strain of the broken bones knitting themselves together again.

"Come in," I said.

He entered carrying my medicine and put it on the
bedside table.

"Thanks," I said, sitting up and taking a pill.

Uncle John sat on the side of the bed and rubbed his
face, like he was thinking of something to say. "You want
to go to church?"

"Not really. Not like this."

"Well, I'm not much of a churchgoer, but I don't have

anything against it either." He looked at me and smiled. "Maybe I'll just cook us a big breakfast. We can sit around here and get fat."

I figured he was trying to be funny, and I didn't feel like laughing, but I gave him a weak smile.

Uncle John took a deep breath. "I want to tell you something," he said. "Something I never told anybody before. Not even your parents."

"Okay."

"You get to be my age and you've never been married, and people get to talking about you. Think maybe you're weird. Maybe something's wrong with you . . . Don't think I don't know that."

"I don't think you're weird," I said.

"I had a girlfriend a long time ago. We were going to get married. She found out she couldn't have children, and she couldn't get over it. She thought she'd let me down. It didn't matter to me at all, but I couldn't make her believe it."

I looked at the floor.

"She left me. It tore me up, and I've never been able to replace her. But, despite that, I've made a good life, Adam. I enjoy my life. It's not real exciting, but I think I've made good decisions. I think I've been a good person. And I have no doubt I can help you on your way to becoming a man."

I nodded. I felt like I would cry if I tried to say anything.

"Just give me a chance, will you?"

Suddenly I couldn't hold it inside any longer. I wanted a parent again so bad. I fell against him and sobbed into his shirt. He put his arms around me and squeezed me closer. We stayed like that for a few minutes without saying anything.

Eventually I pulled away and sniffled and wiped my face with my sleeve. When I looked at Uncle John, he wiped his eyes and I saw he'd been crying too.

"You said I could talk to you," I said.

"Of course you can. I'm right here listening."

"I found them," I said. And I felt some of the pain leave me, like I'd exhaled it.

"You found who?"

"I found my parents."

"What are you talking about?"

"I don't know how to explain it. I need you to take me somewhere."

Uncle John pulled away and looked me in the eyes. "What are you telling me? You found their bodies?"

I wiped my face with the back of my hand and nodded.

"Where?"

"I don't know where it is. I mean, I was there, but I couldn't ever find the place again."

He continued to stare at me.

"It was in the Refuge. Somebody put their bodies in a hole."

"You saw them there?"

I shook my head. "No, but I know they were down there. Their clothes were beside the hole."

"Who put them there?"

I looked at him.

"Who put them there, Adam?"

"Those things."

"What things?"

"Bigfoot."

I saw him wince slightly. I could see he wanted to react but was doing everything he could to keep his composure.

"All right," he said, calmly.

"I don't want you to ask me any more questions about it. I just can't keep it inside me anymore. I want you to know I found Mom and Dad. They're out there buried somewhere. And I know it all sounds crazy, but that's the way it happened and I can't do anything about it and neither can you. But I need you to know."

"Okay," he said.

"And I don't want to go to a doctor about it. I just need you to know."

"Okay."

"And I need you to take me somewhere."

"Where do you want to go?"

"Yellow Jacket," I said.

"Yellow Jacket?"

"It's where I went when I left here. I met a man there. I need to talk to him."

"Is that where you were the whole time?"

I shook my head. "No, I was in the Refuge."

"Alone?"

I nodded.

Uncle John took a deep breath. "Okay," he said. "When do you want to go?"

"Now," I said. "Before it's too late."

35

IT WAS COLD AND RAINY OUTSIDE, SO I PUT ON A STOCKING cap and got into my jacket and pulled an extra sock over my foot on the leg with the cast. Uncle John helped me into his truck, then crammed the wheelchair into the back seat. Then we started out of town toward Yellow Jacket.

We were several miles down the road before he said anything.

"Who is this man? Can you tell me that much?"

"His name's Stanley."

After a few minutes he spoke again.

"Adam, you know we can't just keep it to ourselves if you know where your parents are."

"I told you, I don't know how to find the place again.

It's deep into the Refuge some—somebody carried me out of the woods when I was sick. I don't know where I was."

"But you didn't actually see the bodies?"

"No."

"So, you don't know for sure?"

"I—"

"Forget it. Let's just leave it at that for now."

I nodded.

We drove the rest of the way in silence. What had taken me almost all night to walk only took us a half hour to drive. When we got to the crossroads at Yellow Jacket, I pointed to the left and Uncle John turned onto the dirt road. After a moment I saw the farmhouse ahead of us, and I told him to turn into the driveway and pull up to the porch.

As we approached Stanley's house, I saw that the windows were dark. There didn't seem to be a light on anywhere in the place. I got an uneasy feeling that maybe I was too late.

Uncle John stopped the truck in front of the porch and looked at me. "You sure this is the place?"

I nodded, watching the windows.

"Doesn't look like anybody's home."

"Honk your horn," I said.

Uncle John tapped on the horn. I watched the front door. Nothing.

"Do it again," I said.

"You want me to just go up there and knock?"

"Better not," I said.

"Why not?"

"Because he doesn't like visitors."

"Is he gonna shoot at us?"

"No, they took away his guns."

"Who took away his guns?"

"I don't know. Will you just honk again? Louder this time."

"Crap," he said. He pressed the horn again and held it down for a second.

Suddenly the front door flew open, and Stanley wheeled onto the porch, his eyes bloodshot with rage.

"What the hell!" he screamed. "Get off my property!"

"Good lord, Adam. Is that him?"

I didn't answer. I wondered if this had all been a stupid mistake. I rolled down my window and leaned my head out. Stanley studied me for a moment. Then I saw some of the fire die in his eyes.

"That you?" he said.

"Yeah," I said. "It's me."

His eyes went soft. "Where'd you go?"

At that moment I think I really smiled for the first time in months. "Where do you think I went?"

I don't know how to explain why I felt such relief and happiness. Maybe part of me was just glad Stanley was still okay. But it didn't make sense I would even care about that. And it was more than that. All I know is everything about being there felt like something I'd needed for a long time.

"Is that your uncle?"

"Yeah. He's gonna wait while I come inside."

"I am?" Uncle John said.

"Well, come on, then," Stanley continued. "But I don't know what else I can tell you."

I turned to Uncle John. "Can you help me out?"

He frowned with disapproval. "I guess so. That old man's about a brick shy of a load."

"I'll be all right," I said.

Uncle John got out, and I heard him getting the wheelchair from the back. Stanley watched as he came around to my side and opened my door and set the chair up next to it. Uncle John got me in his arms and lifted me out and set me into the chair.

"What the hell happened to you?" Stanley said.

"Long story," I said.

Stanley motioned toward the ramp at the end of the porch. "Wheel him up here."

Uncle John pushed me to the top of the ramp and then I was able to take over from there. "I'll be in the truck," he said.

"All right," I said. "I might be a while."

"Fine," he said. "Go on."

36

I FOLLOWED STANLEY INSIDE AND SHUT THE DOOR BEHIND ME.

"Didn't think I'd see you again," he said.

"I'm sorry I ran off like that."

"I got a little carried away. All the talking brought back a lot of memories."

"It's okay," I said.

"No, it's not okay. I'm not always like that. I try not to be."

"I know," I said.

Stanley turned and faced me. "So what's all this about?"

I found myself so eager to get the words out, my hands were trembling. "I did it, Stanley."

"You did what?"

I leaned forward. "I went out there. Like you said. And I found them."

"You found what?"

"You know what."

He studied me long and hard. "And they did *that* to you?"

"Yeah," I laughed. "The big one beat the crap out of me. He almost killed me."

"What do you mean? What are you talking about, 'the big one'?"

"I was out there for almost two months. I nearly died. But I found them—or they found me. And I was so scared sometimes, I *wanted* to die. There was the one I saw on the road that night. And I think he had a daughter and a little boy. And then there was the alpha. I called him Alpha. He's the one that almost killed me. And there were more I didn't see very good—but they were out there too. There's at least six or eight of them. They bury their dead, Stanley. They have a hole in the ground, like a cave where they put them. They put my parents in there too. I—"

Stanley suddenly put his hands in the air. "Hold on a second, will you?"

I nodded and found myself catching my breath.

"What are you telling me?"

"I'm telling you I've got the proof."

"You killed one? You got a body?"

I shook my head. "No."

I reached into the pocket of my jacket and pulled out the camera. I wheeled close to him and held it out. Stanley stared at it for a moment, then took it and continued to stare at it in his hands.

"What is this?" he said quietly.

"It's thirty-two close-up pictures of a female Sasquatch. From all angles. She let me take them. I mean, it was like she was posing for me, Stanley. These pictures are like something out of *National Geographic.*"

His fingers began to caress the plastic. "On this camera?" he said.

"Yes. Right there in your hands."

"How? How did—"

"I told you I—"

"Is this a joke?"

I shook my head. "It's no joke. Look at me. This is what it took to get those pictures. And a lot more you can't even imagine."

"No, I know what it takes. But—"

"But I did it. I did it for us."

"For us?"

"I want you to have them. Do what you want with them."

He studied me curiously without speaking.

"Now you have the proof," I continued. "Now you can

stop looking for them. Now we both know they exist, and we can prove it if we want. But the searching is over."

"You don't want to try and show them to anybody?"

I shook my head. "No. But if it makes you feel better, then *you* can. But the search is over."

I saw him start to tear up. And suddenly it was hard to see him as a seventy-year-old man, but more like a kid, like this thing that happened to us reduced us both to the same level.

"It's over," I said again.

"But there's no body."

"No, there's not. We don't need one."

He wiped his face and nodded.

"We don't need one, do we?" I said.

He shook his head. "Not if we have these. Not if they're as good as you say they are."

"That's right."

"Does it help?" he asked. "I mean, do you feel better?"

"Yes, it helps, but not like you think. Now I realize, at least for me, that it wasn't about the proof. It was about having a purpose. I just needed a new purpose. Now I need you to be here for me. You're the only one who understands. I need to be able to call you and talk to you. I need you to get a phone, Stanley."

He looked at the camera again. "How would we even get them developed?"

"I don't know. I don't think it's going to be easy."

Stanley looked up. "What if they're bad? What if the camera didn't work?"

I shrugged. "It's possible. But it's a weatherproof camera. Chances are they're good. The best the world has ever seen."

"So, it's over for you?"

"This part of it is, yeah. And now it's over for you too. But I don't think I'll ever stop thinking about them. And I want to tell you everything I learned."

"They bury their dead?"

"Yes."

"The infrasound?"

"Made me puke and curl up like a baby."

He sort of coughed and laughed with excitement. "A language? Did they talk?"

"I saw it all. There's too much to tell you right now while Uncle John's out there waiting for me. I'm going to come see you whenever I can, but you have to get a phone."

"I can do that."

"And you can call me."

"Yeah, fine."

"Oh, and one more thing."

"What?"

"I lost your boat."

"My boat?"

"Yeah. Your old boat."

Stanley's jaw dropped. "My God, son. To hell with that boat."

I laughed. "I figured you wouldn't miss it."

"I'm going to get a phone," he said. "You have to call me. You have to tell me everything."

"I said I would."

"Okay," he said. "Okay . . . Tell your uncle I'm sorry I yelled at him."

"Why don't you come out and talk to him."

Stanley nodded. "Yeah," he said. "I'd like to meet him."

• • •

On the ride back I felt whole again for the first time in months. Uncle John could sense it.

"You seem happier," he said.

"Yes, sir. I am."

"I don't suppose you want to tell me what all that was about?"

I looked at him. "I want to tell you more than anything. And I don't expect you to believe it all, but I want to tell you."

"Okay."

"I've seen Bigfoot, Uncle John. I know it exists. I can't do anything about that."

"Look, Adam, I'm not one to judge anybody. I know what you think and—well, I suppose it would be miserable for a person to live their life believing in only what they've seen for themselves. I believe in God. He doesn't have me flipping about on the floor, he doesn't even have me going to church very often, but I know he's there. And I guess maybe that's even more of a stretch than an apeman running around in the woods."

"Don't worry, I'm not going to talk about it anymore. Most people won't believe it. I know that."

"Well, I'm not going to go around talking about God to random people either. Folks have their own ideas about things, and sometimes they don't want to think much outside of that."

"I'm going to write it all down. And then I'll let you read it. Meanwhile, I'm going to try and be normal again."

"There's no normal, Adam. There's just you and me and what we decide to make of things."

"Okay," I said.

"So let's get on with it. Me and you. Whatever happens."

"I'm good with that," I said. "Let's go home."

"Yeah," he said. "Let's go home."

EPILOGUE

I go out to visit Stanley most weekends now. Uncle John comes, and he and I have helped Stanley clean up the place, including giving it a fresh coat of paint and hauling away a lot of junk. By now I've told Stanley everything that happened to me, and he even read this. When it came to my experiences with Bigfoot, he helped me make sense of some of it.

I know you're wondering about the pictures. Stanley hasn't developed them yet, and I'm not in any hurry either. He keeps them on the bookcase next to the photo album. I know it's hard to understand, but I think he's come to the same conclusion I did. We've been through enough pain already because of these creatures. If the pictures are as good as I think they are, we'd be asking for a lot more.

Maybe someday.

But no matter what happens with the pictures or anything else, I know I won't ever be the same boy I was before my parents died and before I encountered the creatures. I just can't think of the world the same way anymore. But I think I can be a good version of another boy. A boy who's lonely sometimes. A boy who still has a hard time making friends at school. It's hard to be close to anyone when you have to keep secrets from them. I've adjusted as best I can, and I have other friends now. A few, at least.

I'm starting a website called "Adam's Bigfoot"—a sort of underground blog where people can share their own encounters and talk to people like me to help them make sense of it all and keep them from feeling as alone as we did. That's my new sense of purpose.

Without Uncle John I don't think I could even attempt to come across as normal. He won't ever replace my parents, but he's my dad now. And he's a good one. I still don't know if he really buys into Bigfoot or not. I don't talk to him about it, and it really doesn't matter. I know he understands the creatures are a part of my life now, and he supports me. Most of all, he remains my link to the "others"—what Stanley and I call people who haven't experienced what we have. Because even if you believe, until you meet one of these things face-to-face, you will never understand the effect it has on you.

I think it's possible that one day you might see one of these creatures for yourself. The human population is expanding, and we are constantly driving them out of the forests and into the open. There are more sightings every year. And when the day comes, and your world is changed forever, I'm here to talk to you about it. And tell you you're not crazy at all.

AUTHOR'S NOTE

I have never seen Bigfoot or anything like it. But I did have something happen to me that often has me wondering if such a creature exists. A few years ago, on an afternoon in early December, I was deer hunting on our family farm in a remote part of the Mississippi Delta. This area is mostly cropland, but there are large swaths of dark, swampy marsh with black cypress brakes and impenetrable cane thickets. I have hunted these swamps most of my life, and I'm familiar enough with the woods to walk through them in the dark without a light.

That afternoon I was sitting in a ladder stand fifteen feet off the ground in a hardwood bottom about a mile from the farmhouse. The woods were alive with the cheeping of birds and scurrying of squirrels, all going about their pre-evening rituals of socializing and gathering food. As the sun dropped below the treetops and long shadows fell over me, I settled into my chair in anticipation of dusk, the best hunting time of the day.

About forty-five minutes before nightfall, an uneasy feeling slipped over me. Then it occurred to me that the woods had become completely quiet. I looked around, and there were no more birds, no more squirrels, nothing. Everything had fled or gone silent. The woods felt so suddenly empty, it was unnerving.

Suddenly, I didn't want to be there. Aside from the fact that no deer seemed likely to show themselves, something else wasn't right. I felt like I was being watched. I know from years of hunting that there is a subtle telepathy existing between animals. Imagine being in a room full of people. If you pick a person out of the crowd and stare at them, chances are they will turn and look at you. The same thing exists when hunting. When I am stalking an animal, I try not to look directly at it until it's time to take my shot. Somehow they can sense it.

I grew so uneasy I decided to come down out of my stand and head back toward the farmhouse to see if I could spot a deer while there was still enough daylight to shoot. The woods start getting dark fast once the sun is gone below the trees, so I was going to have to hurry.

I shouldered my rifle and a small backpack of supplies I carried and began walking. The next thing I know, I'm standing at the base of the same ladder stand I had just left. As I said, I know these woods well. This never happens. I was so confused I briefly wondered if I was sick. Then, to make matters even stranger, it didn't seem like the woods had grown any darker. Like maybe I'd never even left. But I distinctly remembered walking and the sound of the leaves crunching under my boots in the eerie silence. But I couldn't actually remember the walk itself. I still can't.

I made it back to the farmhouse that evening and met up with the other hunters. I didn't discuss what had happened to me that evening. I didn't know how to explain it.

Not long after this incident, I was listening to a radio show that was hosting a man who claimed to have seen Sasquatch and was describing his encounter. This man was deer hunting like me, and just before he saw the creature, the woods went silent, like everything scurried away and hid in the presence of this thing. But I didn't connect his experience to my own until he mentioned something called infrasound. This hunter believed the creature emitted a sound that left him disoriented and dizzy. Something like a dog whistle—a sound on a frequency humans can't hear. He suspected the creature used this ability as either a defense mechanism or a weapon. And I thought about the day I was hunting.

Like most people, it is hard for me to grasp such a creature as Sasquatch exists. But I'm overwhelmed by the number of witnesses coming forth every day, claiming to have seen what amounts to a giant, humanlike ape walking on two legs. Unlike most, I have no problem accepting such a creature can live relatively undiscovered in the wilderness areas of the United States. The next time you are in a plane, just look out the window at all the unpopulated forested areas. And I have no problem accepting no remains of such a creature have been found. If Sasquatch exists it is an apex meat-eating predator. In all my years of hunting, I have never found the naturally dead body of a predator in the wild. People often find dead deer and rabbits and other prey but rarely, if ever, a predator like a coyote or bobcat or mountain lion or bear. These animals usually die of natural causes and crawl off someplace remote and hidden to spend their final hours. And within days their remains are eaten by other animals.

But in today's world of trail cameras and drones and a video recorder on everyone's phone, why is there still no compelling evidence of a live one? If all these people are seeing them, why aren't they taking better pictures? Why can't we catch up with this thing? That's the part I have a hard time accepting. But even then, I consider that I've been hunting buck deer for more than forty years. As of today it is estimated there are more than thirty million deer in the United States. I think it's reasonable to assume that if Sasquatch exists, their population relative to bucks would be at least one in a thousand and probably much less. I see fewer than ten bucks a year in the woods. And in all my years of hunting, I've only captured video of one. I recorded it on my phone, and it was so blurry it wasn't worth showing.

In the end I'm left believing there's got to be something more to Sasquatch. I don't know what it is, but I do know there are a lot of people thinking about it. And in this story I give you what some of them say is really going on.

Watt Key
Mobile, Alabama